MW01113605

Terrorists, Traitors and Spies

**Book Two of the Past Generations
of the
Oberllyn Family Chronicles**

By

J. Traveler Pelton

Potpourri Publishing
Mt. Vernon, Ohio

COPYRIGHT

Other Books by Traveler Pelton

The First Oberllyn Family Trilogy: The Past

The Second Oberllyn Family Trilogy: The Present

The Third Oberllyn Family Trilogy: The Future

Family History

In Collaboration with T. Bear Pelton:

Spiritual Works

Dedication

First to God, who is ever my protector and source of creativity.

Next, to my parents and my sister who walked the Red Road before me, and who I will see again someday in the Skylands. I miss you every day.

Finally, to my readers, because a story isn't a story until someone else hears it; it is simply a phantasm, a dream in the maker's head. You make it live when you read it.

A special note to my readers

Many people have asked why I have written this series as I have in three trilogies. As Native American, First Nation's persons, we look back to our ancestors seven generations for honor and lessons; we look forward to the next seven generations that our present actions do no harm: the trilogies represent looking back Seven generations to our forebears, and the present peoples, and the future of our people...so this is written in the traditional storyteller style. I am, after all, a storyteller. I hope you have enjoyed the journey so far, that it has made you wonder what actually would happen if these things occurred. Now let's see where this trail winds...

Family Tree 1910-1985

Youngest Son of Noah Oberllyn was Garrette, who followed in his father's espionage footsteps and founded The Firm.

Head of Family: Garrette Jeremiah Oberllyn; Noah's son married to Genevieve

Son 1   Jerome Jacob Oberllyn; married to Helen Amelia
- Child 1 Daisy Anne
- Child 2 Iris Vivian Iris
- Child 3 Everett Michael

Son 2   Gordon Isaac Oberllyn; married to Virginia
- Child 1 Theodore Oberllyn
- Child 2   Alfred Ian
- Child 3 Angelica Summermoon

Son 3   Grayson David Oberllyn; married to Cora Mae
- Timothy Luke

Daughter 1 Esther Rose; Oberllyn married to Noah Mathis
- Child 1 Clifford Cornelius
- Child 2 Rachel Amethyst and Opal Marie, twins

Son 4 Adam Edgar Oberllyn (adopted grandnephew.), wife Lillian Rose
- Son Glen Donald

The next generation leading the Firm:

Adam, with his son Glen
Jerome's son, Michael followed by his son Noel, married to Violet
Gordon's daughter Angelica Summermoon

And the Next Generation:

Noel's children
- Kai Dante
- Gabriel
- Jasmine
- Lilianna
- Serena
- Micah

All join the Firm as they grow up.

Chapter 1

The train slow-chugged into the platform, hissed and stopped. The conductor helped one family come aboard and the train, water replenished as the family had boarded, rattled down the tracks. The riders carefully made their way to their private first class car with the help of a porter, a car with sliding doors on the adjacent compartments and two benches that made into beds because this would be a long trip. The family stowed their bags overhead and sat a basket at their feet. As they finished and turned around, a short lady with dark brown hair flecked with grey smiled at them from the doorway of the swaying train car.

"Grandma!" exclaimed Daisy. "You have a little train house too?"

"That's right." smiled her Grandma Oberllyn. "This is going to be an adventure for you little ones, I don't believe you've been to California before, and Great Grandpa will have to put you in his Bible."

"I can't wait to meet great Grandpa Noah. He must be in his nineties?" remarked Helen. "I hear he is quite a character."

"Oh, he's got stories to tell, all right." smiled Genevieve. "Garrett's da is 91. Now let me hug these babies and we can settle down. You are all getting so big! You need to come visit me in Arlington. All that Washington air can't be good for you."

"Is everyone going to make it to the reunion this time?" asked her grandson Jerome.

"Family reunion of 1910," smiled his father, Garrette Oberllyn. "Every ten years we go back like lemmings and Da tries to convince us to stay in California. He's worried at how the Firm has grown. But the family lands in California are already divided into farmsteads and every one of them has a

13

family living on it. There simply isn't room without taking from our cousins' land and they need it all. And I don't think I'd be much of a farmer."

"Still, it's going to be nice to catch up and add the babies to our branch of the family tree," said Garrette's wife, Helen. "We'll be adding Daisy, Iris and Everett. Ten years makes such a difference in a family."

"Last time I came in 1900, just after I enlisted, I had no one to add to the family tree." Jerome grinned. "Now look at this group! Are Gordon and Grayson coming in, Mother?"

"Grayson and Cora Mae are already on the train; their bunkhouse is two doors down. The middle one there is for Esther Rose and her family, the one on this side is for Gordon and Virginia and their two little ones," said his Mother Genevieve. "We left the servants home to care for things."

"So Gordon will add Theo and Alfred, and Grayson will add his wife, and Esther will add Clifford and Rachel. Da will have to add pages to the Bible," smiled Helen.

"Be nice to see all the new children in the family. It's going to be a lovely homecoming. Can't wait to catch up with Da. I wonder what the head count will be this time?" Jerome shook his head, smiling at the increase.

"Well, we had 131 in 1890. Forgot how many were in the next one in 1900. We'll pick up Gordon and his bunch somewhere in Indiana," answered his Mother.

"I heard they went to decorate the graves of the ancestors on the old farm."

"I have a roll of paper I want to copy the tree on," said Genevieve. "I want to make a copy for our records out east."

"Good idea. Now I've got a book calling my name back there and want to settle in. You be careful. What time do we go eat?" asked Jerome.

"Dining car is at noon. If we leave about half past eleven, we all ought to be able to eat together. We'll be picking up Gordon tomorrow before lunch."

The families settled into their cars. Grayson stopped by to say hello. Occasionally the sound of a baby crying could be heard, but for most part, it was a quiet trip. At Indianapolis, they picked up Gordon, Virginia and their two children, Theodore and Alfred, and settled in for the long ride to California. The children, all of them small, grew bored, and the parents tried trading them from compartment to compartment to keep them occupied. Having the entire car to themselves was a luxury most folks going to California did not have. It was only a week, and Garrette couldn't help but muse about the original trip west taking six months in wagons. Modern day rail-cars were so much easier but he wondered if they'd be able to fly next time.

Tuesday afternoon, they stopped in Colorado Springs for a two hour layover. Gordon met a tall, thin, well-dressed man on the platform and left with him for a short while, returning in an hour with a box.

"What was that about?" asked Helen.

"I picked up a little something for Grandpa from my friend Nikolai Tesla," he answered. "Da loves inventions and this is one of those corona discharge ozone generators Nikolai patented a bit ago. Nikolai also gave me some info on some of the other things he's working on. He told me about a break-in they'd had. He has officially left Colorado Springs, and is simply cleaning up here. He doubts he'll be back again. His giant coil was disassembled and shipped out already, along with the rest of the lab. He himself is leaving on the train east tomorrow to go to Long Island. Something about building a tower in a secure spot."

"Where did you meet him?"

"Let's see, I believe I met him at the electrical exposition in Madison Square Garden twelve years ago. He had a boat

15

controlled remotely with electricity on display, a model, you understand, but it was impressive. We got into a conversation and he told me what had happened between he and Thom Edison."

"What was that?"

"Appears Thom is a pretty tight operator. He refused to pay Nikolai for some work he'd done after giving his word. Nikolai has had to sue Thom and it nearly bankrupted Nikolai. He's still getting back on his feet and now is headed to Long Island. He's still pretty upset about his house being broken into last night. Said plans for some pretty dangerous equipment was stolen. In the wrong hands, it could be a disaster. The local gendarmes won't do a thing for him."

"That's too bad. Well, we bought some fresh fruit and a few pieces of fabric and we need to get back on board so we know all the children are accounted for."

"Forget the children," remarked Guinevere. "Has anyone seen your father Garrette?"

"Here I am, Mother. Had to send a telegram so someone will be waiting for us at the station," he came dashing up and entered the car. "Now is everyone accounted for?"

After a head count, the conductor called "All aboard!," for any slackers and they settled in for the last part of their journey.

Friday mid-morning, they pulled into Shasta City. They gathered all their things, the men deposited their wives on the platform with the children and went to the rail cars to pick up their trunks. They finished gathering their luggage just as a noisy, self-propelled wagon pulled up, driven by an older gentleman wearing a straw hat and a big smile.

"What on earth , Grandpa?" asked Gordon.

"Grandpa Noah! What is this contraption?" smiled Grayson.

"It's a gasoline powered people mover. It will hold at least twenty five people comfortably on the benches. We ought to be able to get you all in. Mike is following with his horse drawn wagon for your trunks but I wanted you to see what I've been working on."

Helen, Guinevere and Cora looked at each other in dismay as Esther laughed out loud. "I can't wait to try it! Come along Noah, last one in is a rotten egg!" She stepped onto the step stool Noah had set down by the front, climbed in and walked to a bench. She scooted to the end of the bench and opened her parasol.

"It's completely safe," smiled Noah. "I have a steel wall between you and the motor, and there's lots of room, come along."

Slowly everyone climbed aboard, mothers holding babies, men by the wives and all four sons, one daughter, their spouses and children were aboard, just as their cousin Mike came up to load up the trunks. Noah had them all aboard shortly and with a loud toot that startled the neighboring horses, and a popping noise or two, the horseless wagon scooted off towards the Oberllyn settlement across the town and over the river.

Chapter 2

It was a noisy ride back home to the houses. Noah lived in the original log house; there had been repairs and additions through the years, but it was the same one built back in 1855 when the family came to California. Bright flowers grew in the window boxes and the yard, and Grandma stood by the front door, waving as they rode up. She painfully came down the front steps and held out her arms to the children.

"Welcome, welcome," she called out as Garrette gave her a hug. "Was it a hard trip?"

"Nothing like when you came out," smiled her youngest son, born in 1856, after the immigration West. "How have you and Da been, really?"

"Just fine. Your brothers and sisters are all coming over for supper. Just bring those trunks in and we'll settle you all. You're the last to arrive, and all the way from Washington."

"Trains make travel incredibly easy," smiled Helen as she entered.

"And who is this?"

"Mother, this is my wife Helen, and here's Daisy Anne, she's six, and Iris Vivian, she's four, and my son Everett Michael, age 2."

"Such nice looking children!" Ma smiled. "I bet that you all could use a cookie after that long trip?" She led them all into the kitchen, toddlers to small children trailing her like so many baby geese. "Now you said something in your letter about teaching?"

"Yes, Ma, I've been accepted into the engineering staff at Princeton, so we've moved there last month. I'll start teaching in January. It's a change from the embassy for sure, but it's time for little brother to take on those duties."

"Good school, Princeton. You'll enjoy it," commented his brother Joe as he walked in.

After hugs, and introductions, the trunks were moved into a bedroom on the side of the house. The older children were taken out by cousins to meet the animals, and Grandpa Noah took them all on a tour of his workshop.

"You can get all sorts of power out of these gas powered engines. Hard to get enough gas to make them work though."

"They'll always be a place for good draft horses," said old uncle Nathan.

"I suspect so, but you know, none of us are getting younger and the world's moving faster every day. How was that exposition in Chicago you talked about so much in your letters?"

"Funny you should mention it after all these years. Let me get something." Garrette went out and came back with a box.

"This is from my friend Nikolai Tesla. He has all sorts of interesting ideas. Spent an afternoon with him at the exposition where he was talking about alternating current as being the wave of the future. This is one of his machines. It's supposed to be good for you. At any rate, thought you'd like to take it apart and see what makes it tick."

"Is this one of his generators?"

"Not so much; this is supposed to absorb ozone. He calls it a corona discharge ozone generator. His lab was fascinating but he's left and headed for New York. He got hurt bad by Edison."

"Oh? Thom was always a sharp operator."

"Tesla started working for him in 1892 overseas. He came stateside shortly, and worked on problems Thom had with his generators. Tesla fixed them and Edison refused to pay him his bonus. He was banking on it to start his own company, so Tesla took his patents on arc lightening and such and left. The arc patents were worth a lot, and he and Thom are not getting along in any way, shape, or form. At the Chicago World's fair, they had competing booths and everything. Nikolai has a highly trained mind, engineers all sorts of things in his head before he ever writes them down and seldom just tinkers with inventions. Thom depends on lots of tinkering. And Nikolai is really fastidious. Thom-well, you've seen Thom, if it weren't for his wife he'd wear the same clothes for a week. They just don't get along. And Nikolai isn't a very good businessman so he was easy pickings for a sharp like Thom. It's the dreamer in Nikolai. He really needs a wife or a manager."

"Old Thom never was fair with folks. Little too driven and pretty well high on the self-esteem scale."

"What's this, Grandpa?" interrupted Jerome.

"I'm working on something not so high blown as the company you boys keep. That's going to be a really improved harvester when I'm done. Ought to cut down the work of harvesting wheat by at least half. More young folks leaving the farms to go into town and that means farmers need all the help they can get to get the crops in."

"Sounds like a good idea." Jerome mused.

"And what have you boys been doing? I mean besides getting married and raising kids."

Garrette laughed. "When we left here ten years ago, I went to work at the embassy as security. Pinkerton's, as you recall, had gotten me a job. I went to France for three years. I enjoyed that work but with Helen and the kids couldn't justify the danger, so now I'm teaching at Princeton. I like being a professor much better, especially after that bad accident I had protecting the ambassador. Jerome, my firstborn, took my place at the embassy-he's grand with languages, seems to pick them up like the rest of us breathe. "

"Well, after I had learned Chinese from Grandpa, the rest of learning languages was simple. I'll be leaving from here to go back to Arlington and drop off the wife, then I'll be doing envoy duty to Lithuania for a year or so. Things are heating up over there in Europe."

Gordon spoke. "Grandpa, I'm still with the US Marshall's office as a special agent, just like you were for ten years. My wife Ginny wants me to settle down to farming, but I've got a contract to complete first. We all have land adjoining each other in Arlington, and Jerome's wife will be teaching our kids when they're old enough. His wife is a brilliant teacher. " Noah senior nodded.

"That leaves Grayson, still working for the senator's office. His present boss is Thomas Bard, but he may shift loyalties and go into the state department," the old man remarked.

"Why is that?"

"It offers me more opportunities to advance and to see my family." answered Grayson, last to enter. "Thomas keeps us at a frantic pace sometimes and for little reason other than to make himself look busy. I've been doing a few small things on the side; you know how that goes, for the old Agency. The Senator doesn't mind my absences for the State. He actually likes it, I think."

"Adam is studying engineering and applied science at the University of Virginia this quarter. Esther is married to Noah Mathis, who is in the Army Corp of Engineers as a consultant. He has been talking about accepting a call to go elsewhere; he can retire from the army in another year." said Gordon as he poured himself a cup of cold cider from a pitcher left by his Mother.

"Does Grandma still keep bees?" asked Grayson.

"Yes, your Grandma Elizabeth took those over from my Da before he passed back east and now she sells honey all over the valley."

"Wish you could all come to see our places in Arlington. We have a right pretty piece of property, hundred acres each, and hundred in reserve for Adam. Got a good deal on it." Gordon said as he walked around his Father's shop.

"Too far for these old bones," sighed Noah. "Wish my Da was still alive to see how you've all grown up. He was so proud of you"

A gong sounded, sonorously over the valley.

"That's ma, with the gong my pa brought from Chinatown. Works better than a bell to get us all in from the fields. You've got a lot of cousins to catch up on." The men all walked back from the machine shop to the house where the ladies had set food on the old log tables out under the big redwood trees in the front of the homestead. Everyone came and settled onto the benches. Noah held grace and they all dug into their first meal of the reunion.

Chapter 3

The week of visiting whirled by like a ballroom dancer. On Friday morning after breakfast, Noah made an announcement.

"Today we'll hold our joining the family tree ceremony. I have the family tree laid out on Ma's kitchen table. If all of you who have had babies or wives or any other Christian added to the family since you came last to these doors would join me in the kitchen, I want to add them in under your names."

He led the way to a large table that had been set up in the shade of the house. After they were all gathered, Grandpa Noah spoke:

"First, let's remember Joseph Davidson and Nathaniel and Mary Oberllyn, who left this earth to rest in the Lord during this past ten years. Their descendants took over their farms and carry on. Garrette, you left here to go east in 1879. You were a young man when you took the train east to start that career that has led to you working at Princeton. Bring us up to date."

Garrette leaned over the table and looked for his name on the big chart that was unfolded and flat beside the Bible on the table.

"Well, here's my name, youngest son of Noah and Elizabeth Oberllyn born 1856. It's been good to see my brothers who stayed behind. When we left here, Jerome was 9. He finished school and went to work at the embassy as a security person and he met Helen in Greece. They were married, and here I start adding children. His firstborn is Daisy Anne and she

25

is six." He drew in a neat line from his name-one end on him, one Helen, and then lines from beneath it for each child.

"His next child was Iris Vivian and she is 4. His latest child is Everett Michael and he is two." Everyone applauded.

"Gordon Isaac Oberllyn married Virginia Matthews and their children are Theodore Aaron Oberllyn, age 3 and Alfred Ian aged 1." He continued drawing as more applause occurred.

"Grayson David Oberllyn married Cora Mae Smith, and they are expecting their first baby around Thanksgiving time." He handed the pen to his daughter Esther.

"I married Noah Mathias and we have two children Clifford Cornelius age 18 months. Rachel Opal his twin sister, also eighteen months."

"Adam Edgar Oberllyn is still a bachelor, I see," teased Garrette.

"His Da Joe would have been proud of him, just as proud as we are of adopting and raising him after their deaths." answered Noah.

"I'm marrying science and going to go work with Thomas Edison this summer at Menlo Park." answered Adam.

"How did that come about?" asked Jerome.

"He visited the University to talk and he spoke to my professors and they told me I could do an internship at his shop this summer." Adam answered,

"Does he know you don't do Sabbath work?" asked Noah sternly.

"Yes, pa. He acts hard of hearing. Don't know if it's so."

"So no farm for you this summer. Anyway, that catches up the tree," replied his Father, not quite satisfied at this explanation.

"Your other brothers caught theirs up earlier. Look how we've grown since coming from Scotland! Looks like, let me see...over three hundred names on this chart."

"And we are going to sit here and copy out this whole chart," announced Helen. "Then we'll have it on both shores and the family history safe."

"Then I will leave you women to it after we have asked a blessing on all our relations." said Noah. He prayed out loud as everyone owed their heads. Just as he finished, a wagon rattled across the bridge and headed towards the group.

"I have a telegraph for Jerome and another one for Gordon and a third one by golly came in just as I was leaving and it was for Garrette. How'd these folks all know you were all here?"

"Depends who they are, Jonas," responded Noah. "Here Garrette, yours, Gordon, Jerome-hope it's good news." Noah paid the telegraph operator's delivery person and the men opened their telegrams.

Garrette frowned. "Boys, it appears the old agency wants us to join up and meet in Washington."

"Pinkerton's?" inquired Noah. "Thought you were out of that."

"Not exactly Pinkerton's, Pa. Back end of the civil war, a group was founded to be used as needed to help keep the U.S. safe from odd occurrences. It appears we have an odd occurrence and they are having us meet up with some folks in Washington when we get home next week."

"Mine says tomorrow," said Jerome.

"Guess what? We don't fly so it's going to be next week. I need someone to ride into town and send a message back letting them know we don't arrive in Arlington until next week, and won't be available until the following week."

"They be upset over that?" asked his mother Genevieve.

"Not as upset as I will be if they get too pushy. They want our expertise, they best play nice."

"Any idea what the occurrence might be?" his Mother queried. "I really don't like sudden government summons."

"It appears, well, it's hard to put it together but we've had multiple strange fires, storms, and they all seem to have a single apex, sort of a spark that started the whole thing."

"Excuse me?" asked Noah.

"It appears like they start in a specific place each time, and there's a pattern forming." said Jerome.

"Let me explain this. Pa, bad things have been happening for a bit." began Garrette. "For instance, you heard about the assassination attempt on Russell Sage in 1891? It was in the papers. Now not saying he was a particularly loved man, but some of the things Henry Norcross told Sage as he died made Russell call the Agency. Norcross entered Sage's office with a note demanding over a fifty thousand dollars. Sage laughed at him, but Norcross had a bag of dynamite; or at least that's what the papers said. It was not, however, dynamite. It was a device. It did explode, and killed Norcross, wounded Sage, hurt his clerk. What wasn't said was that the note told Sage he had a new form of explosive that would make building railroads safer and easier, more cost effective. Sage was starting on the cross country railroad and it could have saved him a lot of money back then. Sage said Norcross had held up his bag to show him the device when something shiny came through the window and the bag blew. He wanted to know what the shining thing was, said it wasn't just a sunbeam shining through motes. He saw something. He also wanted to know what the new explosive was or the device or what have you. There wasn't enough left in the bag to figure out. The paper in the bag had formulas on it, but it was pretty well shredded and we have only small pieces of it. It sort of looks like Tesla's writing. Tesla isn't one to threaten folks. Sage wasn't going to pay anyone money for an untried invention - and oddly enough, he is still interested in it."

"Well, how are you going to find that?" asked Pa. Jerome shrugged and took up for his father.

28

"That's not the only problem that's in the file, Grandpa. Tesla worked for Edison in 1881 as a consultant, was promised a bunch of money, and Edison saw some of his private works. He thought most were nonsense, meaning not sellable products. He promised Tesla $50,000 if he solved a problem with his DC generator dynamos and when he did, Edison refused to pay. Tesla's room was broken into, and Tesla left shortly after. Edison tried to say Nikolai didn't know how to take a joke. Tesla went off digging ditches to put food on the table but he was able to get funding and started a company making AC motors. However since that time, Tesla has suffered other break-ins. And strange things have happened since he left, some based on greed, some seem to just be someone taking advantage of the moment. In 1892, we had the big labor fight at Carnegie's plant in Homestead and Carnegie pulled in 300 of Pinkerton's men to put down the strike, but an anarchist, let's see, Alexander Berkman, got into the head man's office, Henry Frick, and nearly killed him. There was an unexplained explosion at the plant and a lot of violence, but Carnegie kept the union out of his plants. In 1896, here in California, someone was flying dirigibles around the countryside at night. There were over a thousand reports."

"I heard about that," nodded Pa. "It was in the papers. Didn't see it myself."

"In 1898 the USS Maine suddenly exploded in Havana and we ended up in a short war with Spain. No one knows why it blew up. In 1899 the Great Blizzard hit the country and it was extremely cold. It started on February 11th and it reached -61° F in Montana and -47° F in Nebraska. Snow started falling on February 12th, and Washington D.C. had over twenty inches of snow, with New Jersey getting thirty-four inches. New Orleans was iced over, as were parts of the Mississippi River. By February 14th the temperatures started to rise again. Then just this September, we had the hurricane in Texas, winds 135

29

miles an hour, killed over 8000 souls. Galveston was nearly destroyed. I have reports of all sorts of odd phenomena happening from fires to explosions suddenly happening for no reason the local authorities can find out. The weather reports are alarming."

"Sounds like a bunch of coincidences to me."

"Sounds like the Creator is punishing the country for Wounded Knee." said Grandma quietly. Jerome shook his head.

"Folks I work with don't believe in Creator, Grandma." said Jerome softly.

"I think maybe not coincidences. Remember Nikolai's lab and home have been broken into three times now, and he told me he had plans for different devices stolen. He has a prodigious memory, so he simply rewrote them, and better, but some of those plans were for death ray machines, and weather devices...and someone like Edison who has so few scruples, might have used them, or heaven forbid, one of the Russian anarchists to try and start a revolution here."

"So the President has you looking into it?"

"I and some others. For him to try and call us home so abruptly must mean something else has happened. Well, it will wait. I have three more days with my family and then I am going back." Jerome smiled at his wife. "Helen, don't fret. I don't know that you'd be safer out here with Pa and Ma, but you wouldn't be less safe."

"We have our servants Percy and Sylvester back home, and the dogs and all those things you've scattered around to warn us of folks coming in. I think we'll be fine at home, but I can't help but worry. Besides, you can't protect me from the weather." Helen protested.

"Yes, but I can't help but wonder. Oh, and Pa, the Agency sends its regards." Garrette said quietly. "They tell me you were the best agent they ever had. Course, we all know that."

"It's not the same since Allan passed. And we have our own Firm."

"And the world won't be the same when you pass, Pa. If anyone knew how much this family has gone through to keep everything safe for all the rest...well, it won't happen."

"I'll send the boys in to telegraph our projected date of arrival home so the meeting can be set up. You think two weeks to allow for data collection?" asked Garrette, looking at his sons. "Two weeks it is. Here, Adam, take this to the telegraph person to send back."

"I suppose not," remarked Noah, shaking his head. "We did things different when I was young and Allan alive. However, let me show you this harvester." The men went to study the latest machine to come out of Pa's shop. The ladies all wandered back to the house to visit. The final days of reunion went quickly and it wasn't long until they were once again loading at the train station to go back East.

"I hope they'll be safe." signed Ma.

"I believe they will. We've taught them to survive. The Great Spirit watches over them. We've earned our rest. Let's head back to the settlement." Getting into Pa's horseless carriage wagon, they puttered and popped and banged back to the farm.

Chapter 4

Once home, the family in Virginia settled back into their routine. They had finished the harvest before they left, and all that remained was a thorough fall cleaning of their homes before winter set in. The men met in Washington with authorities briefly, then Garrette met his new class and began teaching at Princeton. He stayed at the farm on weekends and took the train in to teach from Monday through Wednesday. Noah, Esther's husband, retired from the army corps of engineers and worked in the British embassy as a liaison from the United States. Jerome and Gordon, on loan from the US Marshall's office, went back to their offices at the Agency and were soon moving around the country investigating. Grayson went to the senator's office in Washington. He acted as a liaison for his brothers with the President behind the scenes. Adam graduated early and spent a summer at Edison's Menlo facility before deciding to enter the family firm. Time passed, children grew, and in early November of 1913, the men were called again to speak with the President, Woodrow Wilson, and his cabinet.

As was their habit, all six of the Oberllyn men dressed in dark blue double-breasted suits with green and blue striped ties. Garrette, Noah, and Grayson carried briefcases. Jerome, Adam, and Gordon carried walking sticks. They were escorted immediately to the oval office.

"Welcome," remarked Mr. Wilson. "Something to drink?"

"No sir." answered Garrette politely.

"Gentlemen, you have the report we've prepared and sent earlier," began Grayson.

"You don't have the gall to expect us to believe all these disasters are man-made?" demanded the Secretary of State, John Hay. "That's simply preposterous."

"If it were preposterous, we wouldn't be here right now," soothed William McKinley. "I trust these gentlemen, and the government has trusted their family for the last hundred years or so. They are seldom wrong."

"Thank you, sir. If I may continue?"

"We had better get to your reports. I have read, as has my cabinet, with growing dismay, the list of events that have occurred, and which seem to have spread to the continent. Is it your conclusion that the Black Hand has anything to do with this?"

"I can predict the Black Hand will take advantage of the events, but I do not think they are in control. I think we are looking at a more sinister group of people. I have previously sent to you the lists of events that we have found. It appears more certain that the German government has been doing their best to raise a technologically advanced army to conquer Europe, and then I suppose the rest of the civilized world. They have an extensive set of underground spies and appear to be behind the break-in's at several of our own laboratories." He opened his briefcase and took out papers. "Here are some of the messages we've intercepted. Our best guess is that they will target someone in Austria or Hungary and attempt to start the conflict outside of their own country."

"I have intelligence here," said Jerome, "showing the most likely targets and the suspected ramifications."

"I would dearly like to keep the United States out of a European war," remarked the President.

"We may be dragged into it kicking and screaming," answered Noah. "There appears to be a shadow government that is pulling the strings on this, someone deep in the Germanic countries."

"But wild changes in weather, sudden fires, couldn't they all be an act of God?" asked James Wilson, the Secretary of Agriculture.

"In normal circumstances, yes. But coming in such numbers, in such diverse places, around the globe, just as Germany is ramping up her forces and threatening Austria and Hungary, I think not." Answered Greyson.

Secretary of War Elihu Root. Mentioned quietly, "It's I who requested they look into the strange happenings."

"And strange they have been, but how do they fit in with the problems we are facing now?"

"It is our conclusion they are all connected somehow," said Grayson. "There are too many happenings that look too much like what could happen with the device plans that were stolen from our friend Tesla. Without going into trade secrets, he had ideas for devices to change weather, cause fires from a distance, influence people from a distance. I know it sounds fanciful, but many of the devices he has built in the past worked just as he said they would. He's a brilliant man. And if the things were stolen from his lab as he said they were, and if they were in the possession of those in the Black Hand, it could be a tuning up for a war."

The President looked at his cabinet and then nodded at the Oberllyns.

"Thank you gentlemen, for your report. The world as we are used to it is changing faster than we can keep up. Please keep us informed of your progress and we shall have our people look into the Germanic countries for unrest or too much quiet." He sighed and handed a long envelope to Grayson, who passed it to Garrette. "These funds should enable you to keep on compiling data for us within the US. Grayson, you report to me everything that your brothers uncover over the next few months.

I'd like monthly updates if that's possible. Mr. Mathis, I am sending you and Greyson to Europe under special envoy status to find out what is going on in the royal houses. We have telegrams coming to and fro daily from Europe and messengers monthly. Here is the information to get reports directly to us from Europe using the embassy. I wish your father had not gone to his rest last year."

"Noah Sr. was a good man, and loved his country. He was so alert and spry at the last family reunion. He passed peacefully in his sleep, and mother passed a few months later. We keep his high standards." answered Garrette. "But there's not a day we don't miss him."

"Then God speed to you all. Let's try to prevent a war. I pray God our country survives."

"I pray the world is not set on fire," replied Garrette. "May God help us all if we're right."

Chapter 5

Jerome looked up from his building as Gordon entered their hotel room.

"You got it yet?"

"Hanged if I can see how Tesla gets this device to work," he mused. "I don't understand some of his notes and if I don't get it I don't see how some of these ruffians are getting them to work."

"Perhaps we need to send it off to Adam and see if he can do anything with it."

"I'm sore tempted. What did you find out?"

"There is a branch of the Black Hand here in San Diego. Not certain I need to infiltrate it, just document it. Mostly upset Serbs fussing about the new country. Loving their home country, immigrated here, holding grumpy nationals meetings. Any word from the agency?"

"Not at present. Everyone's worrying about the European situation; it's heating up bad. Germany seems determined to force a war or takeover of its' neighbors."

"Blood's not thicker than water over there, I guess. All those royal intermarriages to try and keep peace." sighed his brother.

"I know. Well, the reports from Noah in London are none too promising."

"Yes, Serbia is tired of being under the thumb of bigger countries and their relatives want to join them-that's why the Black Hand is all agitated. Everyone seems to have allied themselves with someone else, almost like they are already drawing lines. Germany and Hungary against Russia, who is with Serbia, Britain and France and Belgium and Japan have treaties, however, France has a treaty with Russia that makes it more confusing. It's like a tinderbox. Noah says it would only take one little incident to make that powder keg blow."

"Well, he also said Great Britain and Germany have both built up incredible navies and that the military is starting to call the shots in government. House of Lords isn't able to hold them all together with tradition. Besides, England is really wanting to keep their colonies in Africa and other countries are eying those. Not good at all."

"Leastwise we'll be able to take a break after this mission. We're supposed to pull back to Washington with the info we have end of June and it's already first of June."

"Hope to tie this all up by the fifteenth and be heading back. Help me look at this diagram, would you?"

Back at Princeton, Garrette was winding up the semester at Princeton by grading term papers. He completed the work, got up, turned in his grades and headed for home. On the train, a gentleman sat down next to him and took out a newspaper. "Am I right in supposing I speak to Garrette Oberllyn?" He said softly as he opened his paper.

"Yes, I'm Dr. Oberllyn. And you, sir?"

"I am but a messenger. I have a newspaper for you from a friend. You need to read the article on page 5. Then you need to talk to your people. He will be in touch." He handed Garrette a newspaper he took out of the folds of his coat, then folded his own paper, got up to leave. "You will find it an interesting article."

"I am sure I will. Are you certain you can tell me nothing else?"

"Not at this time. Nikolai says hello." The gentleman left for another car, leaving a bemused Garrette holding a folded newspaper. *Well, I am not going to open this on a crowded train. Hard telling what's on page 5. I'll wait, and open it from a distance just in case.*

At the Virginia farm, Mother and the daughter's had gotten all the early crops in, and were canning into the late afternoon. Spring cleaning had been completed, school had gotten out, and the menfolk had finished the practice range the weekend before. The ladies planned to make good use of it once they got the peas completed today.

Knowing that the men should be home soon, they were all hurrying to get ready for supper together. Unlike most families of the day, everyone ate together in the big dining room, the children had their own table, but could hear what was said. Their parents thought it was good training for them. Nanny was scandalized. As soon as you were six, you got to move to the dining room. Those under six ate earlier upstairs in the nursery. When you reached 12, you joined the big table.

"Just two more canners full and we can clean up," sighed Helen. "I really feel like shooting tonight."

"I'd like to get rid of some of my frustrations as well," remarked Ma. "There, that's the last sauce coming out." The women quickly washed out the remaining canner, wiped down the counters and left the maids to complete the clean up and get supper on. Ma and her four daughters all went out to the shooting range.

Chapter 6

"What's that smell?" Gordon wrinkled his nose and fanned the air as he entered the hotel room.

"One of the ingredients for the death ray is an extract from musk. Only musk I could get here was from those two skunks over there. I put them to sleep and milked them so I could extract the musk safely and put it to distillation. I guess after the first few drops I couldn't smell much anymore."

"You mind if I open a window?"

"Must have dropped shut while I was working, yeah, good idea." He went back to work at the plans. "Now, if I add sulphur to this ..."

Jerome looked at his brother.

"You know, back in 1888, when Noah was in Europe the first time monitoring Wilhelm's succession to Kaiser in Germany, he felt that there was a lot of animosity there. What do you think if perhaps we are thinking too much of the Black Hand thing and not enough to what's behind some of the other activities of that government?"

"What do you mean?" quizzed Gordon.

"You know, 1888 was a really interesting year. In our own church, the big meeting over righteousness by faith nearly tore the congregation apart. A.T. Jones and his friend Wagoner presented messages that upset all the brethren, being backed up by Sister White, and she ended up in Australia."

"Yeah, so? It ended up for the best. We now have a well-established work in that country. The dear lady is safe in California now."

"And Wilhelm came to the throne and some of his first actions were to declare himself Supreme War lord and amp up his generals? He keeps making those speeches and firing up his people, while on the other hand saying he doesn't want war."

"I think we all know it's a given he is going to try and make this war happen."

"I know, and Noah is back in Europe trying to get a handle on the feeling of the people. His last report says he isn't sure of the Black Hand."

"Didn't Wilhelm say that Czar Nicholas of Russia and he are cousins?"

"Yes, and they've been sending telegrams back and forth for some time now."

"I sure don't like the sounds of that shaping up."

"We best keep an eye on it. Now, let's look at this machine. What did Tesla call it?"

"He said three machine plans were taken from his lab, a death ray, an earthquake device which he thinks has already been used to cause the San Francisco earthquake and to sink the Titanic, and some sort of mind alteration device. This is supposed to be the death ray. I can't make heads nor tails of some of his ideas."

"Well, the incidents do fit into the time line of when his plans were stolen and they did cause damage." looking back to the plans, he sighed. "He does make interesting notes."

"Well, if the earthquake machine is in operation, it could cause no end of difficulty."

"Well, so could Wilhelm. At least I understand most of his ramblings. Say, if you studied the earthquake device we are pretty sure works, could it help you understand this one?"

"One better. I'm turning Adam loose on it as soon as he arrives. He's worked with Edison and finished his engineering degree; I suspect he'll understand this better."

"He comes in at noon. It's nearly that now. I'll go meet him at the station."

"And I believe I'll send a telegram to Noah."

The two men went out.

Gordon went to the telegraph office and quickly sent out a message to Noah. "Noah Mathis: Watch Serbia. BH pullback, Caution advised, safety plan in place for you/yours. GO" he paid the operator and headed for the train station.

As he got closer, he checked his watch as he heard the train pull in from several blocks away.

When he heard gunshots, he started to run. He came upon a scene that seemed surreal for all of a second as he took his bearings, got into a position behind some trunks and returned fire.

His brother Jerome was on the ground, rolling for cover. Adam had climbed to the top of a box car and was lying flat to make the smallest target available. Two people were lying on the ground, others were still inside screaming.

"What the devil, Jerome? All you had to do was pick up Adam?" He called.

"And I almost did when three men jumped aboard and started firing. I have no idea if it's a hold up or what."

"Adam's up top. Do you know if he's hurt?"

"I don't know, but one of the men tried to grab him and was dragging him to the front of the car: Adam objected to being used that way. When the men started shooting at passengers, he got free and jumped overhead. He pretty well incapacitated the would be kidnapper on the way up. Don't know if they were going to use him as a shield or if he was the object."

"We'll assume he's the object. If we remove the object, we may be able to stop the carnage." Gordon said.

Just then a sheriff and deputy joined them.

"What's going on?"

43

"We think it's a robbery. People inside are hostages. Don't know who the robbers might be."

"Well, we need to stop this. Folks are getting hurt. Any word on what they want?"

"Nobody has said anything." Just then, from inside the car, a man called out.

"We don't want to hurt anybody else. Just give us the man we came for, three fast horses and we'll go."

"What man?" yelled the sheriff. "You already shot a couple out here."

"And for every minute you delay, we'll shot another and toss them out."

"What man?" yelled Gordon.

"We need a young man supposed to be on this train named Adam Oberllyn. He has something we need and we'll just take him and go."

"That's our little brother, sheriff. I don't know who these men are but Adam just came back from school. He couldn't possibly have anything they want."

The sheriff eyed them cautiously. "I don't want any more shooting. We don't know who it is in the car that's doing the shooting. Can't rush the car that I can see."

"No, but maybe we can flush them out," said Jerome.

"How we going to do that?" The sheriff looked dubious as he watched the train.

"I got an idea. Try to delay them, sheriff, while Gordon runs back to the room for something. He'll bring back three horses so it looks like we're cooperating. You keep the robbers talking to you."

"This better work."

"Hope so."

"This is Sheriff Bateman. We don't want anyone getting hurt. I've sent a man for some horses. Now who is this person you're looking for?"

"He's a tall thin boy, about 20, just got back from university, has a carpetbag with him and a case. We need him."

"What you want with him?"

"Never you mind. You get him."

"If he was on the train, is he still there?"

"No, he ran off after breaking my brother's leg here. He went out the other side. You got to find him. We need him now. And we need the doc for my brother's leg."

"You going to hurt this young man?"

"No, we just need him. Our boss says he's real smart and he wants to hire him for a job."

"Your boss always kidnap the people you want to hire?" asked the sheriff speculatively as he stood up to get a better look.

"He wouldn't come with us gentleman like so we had to try and persuade him." replied the kidnapper.

"Can we get help to the people lying out there you shot?"

"You for sure bringing the horses?"

"Yes."

"You can move the people and put the horses over here by this door. You sending someone for the doctor?" he paused. "How are you going to find Oberllyn?"

"He's not over here, and you shoot at whomever comes out of hiding. How do you expect us to find someone? He's most likely in the bushes on the other side of the station. He's not in the station back here. As for the doc, we don't call him until the shooting stops. Not risking the only doctor in miles on a gunfight til it's over."

"My brother needs a doctor."

"No doubt. This Oberllyn anything like the rest of his family?"

"What do you mean?"

Just then, the sheriff noticed both Jerome and Gordon had left the horses tied by the train as the men specified. On the

45

opposite side of the train, bricks were thrown through windows and much cursing ensued, followed by a few gunshots and two men being tossed out the door. Gordon was on the roof, and helping Adam down the back side.

The sheriff stood up, he and his deputy with their guns drawn.

Three men were on the ground, gasping and shaking.

"Can't breathe," gasped one.

"Lordy, what is that stuff?" Other passengers were coming out of the train car, also red faced and gasping.

Jerome came from behind the car.

"It won't kill you but you may not be able to smell for a while. It's skunk musk. The two skunks are loose in the train car, mad as hornets at being woke up and flung through windows so you'll need to give them a while to simmer down. Those men are your kidnappers-I got them each with a full grown skunk to the face so it may take a while for them to breathe. I'd suggest getting their weapons and locking them up pretty quickly."

"That the man they were looking for?"

"Yes sir. My name is Adam and I just returned from working with Thomas Edison. They must have thought I had information on secret projects or something."

"Did you?"

"No sir, I just acted as his go-fer all summer. I fetched things, carried, cleaned, you know, what they always do to interns. I was on my way here to meet up with my brothers and these men told me I was supposed to go with them to meet their boss and when I wouldn't and the train pulled into the station, they grabbed me and started to haul me off. I kicked my way free and got out the other side and climbed on top. I had no idea they would start shooting people."

"They mention who this boss was?"

"I don't think so; they said something about my special talents being need by black hand or something like that, maybe it's an Indian tribe?"

Jerome's eyebrows went up. He slightly shook his head. Adam continued, "Anyway, thank you for rescuing me, sir." he turned a little white and shaky. The injured were being carried to the doctor. "Are they going to be ok?"

"Doc will deal with them. I don't want to be unfriendly, but maybe you boys better pull out of town."

"It was my thought as well. We'll go pack our things."

"Man, Bill, whatever they got hit with, how we going to keep them in the jail?"

"We'll put them in the back cell together. You can be on foot duty for a few days so you don't have to come in. "

"I don't even think tomatoes are going to cut that smell."

Doc stood up. "His leg's not broke, he's got a good sprain is all. He'll need to stay off his feet for a few days with it elevated. You boys give him a couple shots of rotgut and he'll sleep. He'll feel better when he wakes up."

"Yeah. Well, until he realizes he's in jail. Let's get them locked up, Mac." He jerked the men to their feet, grimaced and told them to walk in front of him, the brother with the sprain between them, supporting himself on their shoulders. Once at the jail, he locked up two of the brothers, then gave a half glass of whiskey to the hurt brother and sent him into the cell to lie down. Locking the door, he went out, shut the door to the jail and went out to wash up.

"Bill, those Oberllyn's must have an interesting time of it to be carrying skunks around."

"Doubt they have much of a social life," muttered Bill as he tried to wash up at the pump.

Chapter 7

Garrette got off the train, the paper under his arm and started his daily walk home. He enjoyed this end of the day, the twilight coming on, everything slowing down. He passed the last house and came to a stream, crossed the bridge and stood on it, then sat his case down and withdrew the newspaper. He checked it thoroughly, felt it for odd lumps. It appeared to be the back section of the times, nothing more. He slowly opened it, found page five. Several ads were marked by someone before he got the paper. Under help wanted, "Need an honest, young man, preferably with engineering degree, to work on several bridge projects. Inquire at Bachman office with letters of recommendation." Under real estate, "For sale or lease, large farmhouse on 49 acres, fenced, orchard and berries mature, two barns, woods, stream. Can be seen at 143 Avondale lane." That startled him as that was his address and his farm in the for sale column. Shaking his head, he read the next marked ad, this one under farm misc. for sale, "Two pair of large, well trained Belgium horses, trained to pull, $600 per pair. 40 head of Shetland Sheep, wonderful fleece, docile, entire herd $800. contact farm at 143 Avondale Lane."

In the personal ads was listed, "Four widows looking to meet Christian gentleman to replace recently deceased husbands. Have farms and children to care for and looking for good men." Garrette began to get a creepy feeling, as if someone was looking over his shoulder and he couldn't help looking up and around his perimeter. He saw penciled in at the bottom of the paper, "See obits."

He turned back to page two and saw pictures of himself, his sons Jerome, Grayson, Gordon, one after the other, with day of birth and day of death Tuesday of next week. He checked the newspaper, realizing it couldn't possibly be the real Times, and turned back to read his obituary curious as to how he was going to die. According to the obituary, the beloved husband of Genevieve was suddenly taken from her by an accident that occurred while out of town. Why in heaven's name would Nikolai send him this? It was far from a joke, considering what they were getting into lately. He perused the rest of the paper for clues, then quietly folded it up and put it in his case and walked the rest of the way to the farm. Standing soon in front of its gate, looking at the roses blooming over the porch, the trumpet vines climbing the trellis, the clematis in full purple and pink bloom, he shook his head. It was a pretty picture and getting killed in four days was not something he liked to contemplate. They were going on a trip to meet up with other operatives: someone knew the itinerary. He supposed Adam was the man listed in the want ads. He was supposed to come home in two days with Jerome and Gordon. Adam was going to stay with his Mother and the farm while the other men were gone on their trip to Europe. It was a threat but a well thought out one, by someone who knew their itinerary.

He entered his gate thoughtfully and headed in the front door to meet his wife Genny.

Chapter 8

"Is the packing about done?" asked Noah as he entered their suite of rooms. "I can remember when packing was one suitcase and a bag." He shook his head as he saw the trunks and boxes, bags and cases in a pile on the hotel bellboy's dolly.

"Back then you weren't so high up in embassy circles," smiled his wife. "And one trunk is just the things I got for the layette just in case it's needed before we get home."

"How are you feeling, wife? Are you up to the crossing over to Austria?"

"As long as the channel cooperates with us, we should be fine. I can't have more morning sickness than I already have."

"Well, we will shortly be back in America. This trip to Austria is just to give them greetings from the Queen and a few messages from the brothers. It ought not take long."

"How much not to be spoken about work is there?" Esther whispered.

"I have to find out who the target is for the attempt if I can. We know there is a coup planned. Wilhelm is making so much bluster that the people are restless. I am glad the twins are home with Grandmother."

"Yes, thank God for Genevieve." she stepped back from his embrace. "There! That is the last bag, some gifts from England for our children and Mother. Let's go to the ship and get settled."

"The ambassador has decided not to come into Austria, so I'm heading the delegation. The ambassador is going direct to Serbia. If all goes well, we ought to be home by June 15."

"Baby is due in September, so we ought to be just fine."

The entourage Noah had traveling with him included his wife, attaché, and a maid to help his wife. They were traveling as ostentatiously as possible, for safety's sake. The embassy packet he was carrying to Franz-Joseph of Austria/Hungary contained information on the recent strange happenings he and the family were working on, warnings of danger, and the possibility of what side the US might have to take if hostilities increased. There were the inevitable balls and dinners to go to as a representative of the US government, and then he ought to be able to get his wife and go home to Virginia and relative safety. He boarded the ship with his group and went to his cabin to study missives from his brothers.

Esther lay down for a rest and the maid hung up things to drop the wrinkles before the dinner with the captain this evening.

He read and scrutinized the letters for what they didn't say. After a while, he sighed and closed his eyes to think.

"Way too many coincidences. I need to locate the Black Hand operational base as quickly as I can and ascertain the target. I doubt it is anyone of too much consequence; I think it's going to be used as an excuse for war; how little our excuses for war have been! It's as if we were born to be a bloody race of malcontents and monsters. At any rate, Esther should be safe in the embassy; Stephen and I can do the reconnaissance the first couple nights and hopefully get the victim into a safer situation so nothing happens. I can't wait to be heading back to America."

Esther slept on for an hour and didn't notice the ship pulling out of port. The maid finished her work and with Noah's permission, left the stateroom to go out to watch the sea for a few minutes. Stephen, his aide, came to the door.

"I think I may have overheard something," he said quietly.

"Come in, man. What is it?"

"The archduke of Austria is making a trip shortly to visit Bosnia. Several Germans are making a deal of it for some reason downstairs. Austria and Hungary signed that pact of cooperation a couple weeks ago, you recall? It appears they may be making overtures to Serbia and Bosnia, sort of joining up the smaller nations into a united field."

"Interesting."

"Nicholas Hartwig, the Russian minister, was murdered yesterday while visiting the Austrian's legation. Odd that the Archduke choses a day just before to leave and be gone when the murder occurs."

"Yes, that is troublesome."

"The Kaiser is pretty upset about it, but he knows the Austrians and Hungarians are trying to provoke a war."

"Yes, and we are all trying to stop it."

"Do you think we'll succeed?"

"I honestly don't know. It's heating up badly. I'd like to keep the US out of it if that's possible."

Just then Esther stirred.

"Noah?" she asked.

"Stephen and I were just discussing...Babe Ruth, dear. He has his first game with the Red Sox tomorrow."

She sat up and yawned. "That's good, dear. And I wasn't born yesterday, you two. Baseball season isn't for weeks. What's really going on?"

"Just trying to stop a war."

"Well, I think on that happy note, I want a walk around the deck. Is Maryann out there?"

"Yes, but I want to stretch a bit too before dinner. Let me accompany you. Good work, Stephen," he said in an aside. "Keep circulating."

Chapter 9

Adam, Jerome and Gordon arrived home by Saturday from their trip, adding to the list of coincidences their research on the death ray and the report on the attack. They gave Adam the plans they'd received from Tesla, who seemed to be in heavy negotiations with the British government, Prime Minister Chamberlain, about something using fireballs that was supposed to protect the British people from attack.

"At any rate," Adam said "Tesla's busy and not inventing something dangerous right now, least I don't think he is. If we can decipher this stuff, we might be able to get something useful. What is that smell? Musk? As in skunks?"

"Long story." replied Jerome.

"But his field never was chemistry. It's engineering."

"Maybe I read it wrong?" Jerome answered, stepping back a little.

"My thoughts exactly. I'll take this info over to the lab and get started on it."

Adam muttered to no one in particular, "Very day I thank my lucky stars that Edison is so very commercial. There's no money to be made in munitions or he'd be in that instead of electricity."

"Well, if Tesla doesn't stop fighting with Marconi," began Jerome.

"Yes, yes, I know. Can't those boys all just get along?" asked Genny, their Mother, coming in the room. "Now we need some help on the shooting field."

"Excuse me, Mother?" asked Gordon.

"Somethings' going haywire with that new parasol gun and I'll not have it blowing up in my face if I have to use it sometime."

Gordon smiled. "Mother, you do surprise me. You ever have normal the stove doesn't work type problems like other Mothers?" He took the parasol and started to take it apart.

"Where's the fun in that? Oh, and you all got telegrams from Woodrow."

"Greyson ought to be taking care of those."

"I think he is, but the President needs reassurance. Wish Noah and Esther were back."

"He'll be here in under a fortnight," remarked Genny. "in the meantime, have you gotten what the government needs together?"

"Just that I'm pretty sure it's not the Black Hand. I think they're tools. There; the parasol's all ready for checking out. Just needed an adjustment, Mother," remarked Gordon. "Shall we go test it?"

"Excellent work." remarked her husband. "Wife, a word. What's happening next Tuesday?"

"Tuesday? Nothing I know of, the dinner party over at the Bronson's is Wednesday. Why do you ask?"

"Nothing right now dear. Just can't help thinking I'm forgetting something."

"Have you been out to see those horses you bought? Can't imagine taking that long trail west using them to pull, but bet they could. Such lovely animals."

"Yes, it's a family legend in the making." he drew in a breath. "Let me just go read my telegram, and get dressed for dinner."

"Sounds like a plan. Let me shoot this a couple times and I'll go in to oversee that dinner." She turned towards the targets, drew up her parasol and fired three bullets. The made a little oval shaped hole in the target.

"Nicely lined up in the center, wife."

"Yes, the scope is all straight now. I'll need to be careful."

"Let me take it and clean it for you."

"Thank you. And I'll see you at dinner." Genevieve trotted off at her usual quick gait, smooth but fast, headed for the kitchen, stopping occasionally to pick a flower from the gardens she passed. Garrette watched her with a thoughtful smile.

"She doesn't really look like a widow yet. Let's hope the events Nikolai tried to warn me of do not come to pass."

Just then, his boys came in.

"Father, what do you think of the message you got?" Jerome spoke as he walked up to Garrette, along with his brother Gordon.

"Hadn't read it yet. Let me see."

"I wonder if Grayson got a similar missive."

"I don't know. Let's compare notes. I'm to come to The White House for further orders on Monday."

"Same as us. He's calling us to a special meeting? Does Greyson know?"

"Do I know what?" came a voice.

"The meeting Monday?"

He studied the three telegrams. "No, I just got told that the President wants me to make a visit to Edison at the lab in Orange Park; something about search lights. I've heard it's a pretty amazing place, larger than Menlo Park."

"So you'll be out of town Tuesday."

"Yes, I'm supposed to be there Tuesday. Is there a problem?"

"Come into the library. I want to show you something."

In the library, they all perused the newspaper purportedly from Nikolai.

"Something odd is going on. If we go to the White House and are asked to go to somewhere on Tuesday, we might not want to go," said Jerome.

"Agreed. Especially if the travel plans are made for us." replied Greyson.

"No, if the plans are ready, we take them, but we change them. And we go forearmed with information that might just make for some interesting changes in these plans," replied his Father.

"And I have to find out who the traitor is in the White Houses" said Gordon.

"That is an excellent idea. We'll reconvene here afterwards when Noah returns from his journey. It doesn't appear Adam is a target."

"Who's the Bachman group?" asked Adam.

"Unknown. They aren't listed as a business anywhere; no research lab or college by that name. I thought to run it past Woodrow and his cabinet."

"Can we call the old agency and have them do a little research?"

"Won't hurt. I hear Alan's protégé is doing well. There's the bell. I think it's time for dinner. And boys, don't get your Mother all upset over this."

"She does like to run off a bit, doesn't she?"

"She has a pretty short fuse on this sort of thing lately."

Chapter 10

Noah danced with his wife at the reception.

"They really know how to create elegance here on the continent," she mentioned.

"Too bad it covers up a basically rotten core," said Noah.

"Never knew you to be so glum."

"I'm going to leave you here at the reception. Steven and I have a short trip to take together. We'll be back quickly. I have to make a delivery and this covers it pretty well."

"I shall simply keep dancing."

"Don't tire yourself out."

"Rather dance than talk to all the young biddies," she smiled over her shoulder. "They chatter like old hens, picking each other's clothing apart. Like you said, rotten core. But very pretty to look at. Be safe."

"Stay inside unless you are accompanied by known allies. Steven is waiting at the wall."

"Don't muss your clothes," she ordered. He laughed quietly. "Not to worry." The music ended, he bent over her hand to kiss it and led her to her next partner as she had consulted her dance card.

"Count David, please take care of Esther for me? I am called to a message."

"I shall endeavor to not exhaust such beauty in dancing." The music began and he bowed over her hand. Noah watched a moment and stepped outside, removing a cigar from his vest as if to go smoke. Once out, he slipped out the garden hedge and walked quickly to meet Steven who was dressed in black. He took overalls that covered his tuxedo and slipped it over his clothes, covering his face. They slipped out through the hedge and walked quickly to where two horses were tethered, got on and rode off towards the warehouse district.

They rode in silence for the first mile, then Steven came alongside his colleague.

"Maybe next time I can be the ambassador and you the servant?" he said. "I never get to dance."

"There's more danger in the dancing than in delivering messages," smiled Noah. "As long as our friend is waiting, this ought to be simple."

"Yes, as long as he shows. Have you been listening to the news?"

"Through back channels."

"The Archduke is making rash statements that many are taking umbrage to; and he has appeared several times to his people to be whipping up interest in joining the military."

"Serbia as well? That bodes no good. Here's our corner."

They dismounted. "It appears that the iceberg that struck the Titanic two years ago wasn't really large enough or hit properly to cause it to sink."

"There were many targets on board that ship," remarked Noah. "It was foolish for all of them to get on an untried vessel just for fashion. Too many died."

Steven nodded. "There is word from others that the people aboard that survived heard a loud noise, a jolt, and then confusion as the ship was sinking. Some report a huge flash of light off the bow. One described it as a fireball."

Noah's eyes went up. "Really?"

"Our mutual friends have carefully questioned the survivors. There are interesting stories among them. Many heroes of course, many good people." He paused as if collecting thoughts. "Word that Ireland is trying again for independence is starting to trouble people."

"Almost as much as the Balkan states."

"Agreed on that. That might be our man over there."

A young man, walking with a cane, approached, driving a horseless carriage. He pulled to a stop by the two men. The horses, used to such contrivances, did not shy.

"Evening, brothers," said the young man jovially.

"Greyson? What are you doing here?"

"White House sent me over two weeks ago. Special envoy from the President."

"So you're not our contact?"

"He met with an accident that looks all too planned. I'm coming back with you. Tie the horses to the car, let's go back to the ball. We are all to leave in the morning. The Firm needs us home."

"The Ambassador was supposed to get this information," began Noah.

"The Ambassador has been recalled. In spite of all our Secretary of State has been doing, war is going to happen. We've discovered the target and we can't stop it. Our job is to try and keep the United States out of it. So we leave in the morning."

They rode in silence. Greyson handed a note to Noah who read it quickly, gave it to Steven who also memorized it, then set it on fire with a match. He dropped the remains as they drove by. Noah removed his overalls, brushed back his hair as they arrived at the ball, packet still in his vest pocket. He and his brother came up the front steps together. Steven drove the automotive back to the area designated for the vehicles, and left it. He stepped behind some bushes, changed clothes and went up the steps himself.

61

The three men entered the ballroom, all looking unruffled, all dressed in matching tuxedos, looking for Esther. She came up on the Duke's arm.

"Husband! Back so soon, and Greyson?"

He bowed over her hand.

"So good to see you again, Esther." He smiled. "And Duke, how good of you to take care of Esther for us. World events being as they are, it's good to have some friends."

"I thought you were serving the President in the White House?" asked the Duke.

" It was decided I might be best here. The Irish problem and all that sort of thing."

"Ah, yes, the Irish. Quite the problem. What do the colonies think we ought do?"

"Diplomacy is always the first action. In fact, we'll be sailing tomorrow to go to Ireland to lend support."

"That's good of you."

"But now I just want to dance with my lovely sister. I don't get to see her often. Esther, if I may?" Greyson took her hand and they stepped onto the dance floor. He swept her away into a slow waltz.

"Greyson, what are you really doing here?"

"There's a spy in the White House. Woodrow is in trouble. The family is being recalled back home but first, we must get out of this country. We aren't safe. We're going to stay about another half hour and then use your delicate condition to leave. Noah and I have some things to do tonight and we need you and your maid to have everything packed to go onboard the ship taking us home when we return. I'll have a wagon outside the residence in two hours to take out your things. We'll meet you at the dock."

"What's going on?"

"Too many ears here, sister," He smiled and nodded at dancers going by. "Just be ready to get on the boat by midnight."

Chapter 11

Garrette, Gordon and Jerome went to the White House as requested. They sent Adam and the rest of the family by train to visit with friends in Atlanta.

"Adam isn't with you?" asked the Secretary of State as they entered the Oval Office.

"He's on an errand. And how are you, Mr. Bryan?"

"More than a little discouraged. I've got 28 treaties signed, trying to keep world peace and Wilhelm simply refuses to speak to us."

"He really doesn't want peace. He wants to fight Victoria for world dominance."

"For heaven's sake, Garrette, they're related by marriage."

"Victoria sold off her children all over Europe by marriage to try and keep the peace, and blood ties don't matter. It's more like the children are hostages to their mate's countries."

"What would be our stance if some of them asked for asylum?"

"That would be a sticky wicket," replied the President. "I appreciate the work Williams' done. However, we aren't here for that. What else have your folks discovered about the increasing catastrophes? Are they coincidence?"

"In our considered opinion no. It can be ascertained someone has figured out some of Tesla's weaponry. They've also gotten together some pretty horrible gases to use and have stockpiled them and other weaponry. They appear to be just looking for something to light the powder keg."

"I do not want America in a war!" said the President. "This last information I received about the Titanic, do you think it's true?"

"Unless we can dive deep enough to pull up the hull, all we have are eyewitness reports of a fireball and an explosion, and then the iceberg."

"With this mess in Mexico going on, we simply can't go off halfcocked into a European conflict."

" I believe, sir, that's is exactly what Wilhelm is counting on."

One of the Cabinet members spoke up. "An assassination would do it. The right person at the right time, tempers flare." He shrugged his shoulders.

"We think that is exactly what is planned," began Garrette. "Right now, the smaller states are trying to put together treaties defending each other; they can see what Germany is doing and they're uneasy. However, they don't trust each other. In the meantime, all of this is distracting us from the testing going on in our own country. From the Titanic going down to four days of rain in the Miami Valley flood the region and mark the worst natural disaster in Ohio's history, killing over 360 people and destroying 20,000 homes, the temperature in Death Valley, California, hits 134 °F, the highest on record; the Great Lakes Storm of 1913 kills more than 250 and those are just the weather events. Our country is woefully unprepared for the type of war that Wilhelm has planned."

"Which is another reason we need to stay out of it."

"I know. But what would make us join if it occurred?"

The President thought long and hard. "Garette, they'd need to attack us physically, personally, before I'd enter. I will not sign treaties of mutual protection."

"A world controlled by the German war machine would not be a good one to live in."

"I know that. I just don' t think we need get involved, when we have Mexico still frothing at the border." He paused. "Now, what we want is for you and your people to be our eyes and ears. I've already sent Greyson to go get Noah and bring him home early."

"What?" said Gordon. "We didn't know he was being recalled."

"He's not exactly. I just think all of you here working on this and finding out who is using Tesla's inventions and stopping them is of greater import than us getting involved overseas. I've half a mind to recall all our embassy personnel until it calms down."

"Mr. President, is it wise to take all the diplomats out at this juncture?" asked the Secretary of defense. "Isn't that sort of a vote of no confidence?"

"I didn't see them coming over here to help with the Mexican conflict. They need to take care of their own affairs. The agreements we have keep at least 28 of them from attacking us. I doubt the others will. Garrette, stay behind a moment." The President dismissed them all with a wave of his hand. Garrette stayed seated."

"Garrette, I don't want the others to know that I'm sending you and your people out on special assignment. They think I just called you all home. I didn't."

"You did call Noah and the others home to the US."

"After they've delivered information to the British embassy, yes. I expect them home in ten days. I want you and Jerome to go Edison's new lab and enlist his help in the effort to build our defenses,. I want his suggestions on how to build up the war machine quickly in case it should be needed. I want Adam and Gordon to go to Tesla's lab and do the same thing."

"So Orange Park and New York?"

"Yes, and what do you think of this young fellow in Germany? My science people are going over the wall about his theory of relativity."

"Einstein? My friends at Princeton are actively watching his progress. Such a brilliant man."

"My people are arguing about it. Some saying brilliant, some nonsense."

"Time will tell what he does. When do you want us to leave?"

"As soon as is possible."

"We will leave Thursday. If we leave immediately, it will look too suspicious."

"Three days then."

"Good day, Mr. President."

Chapter 12

Noah, Steven and Greyson left their tuxedos in the car and donned the dark over clothes best donned for night work. Going back to the embassy, they quietly moved in and laid a packet on the ambassador's desk.

Similar missives went on other desks that night. At one, they met back on a familiar corner where they were met by a tall, thin man.

"Greetings, comrades."

Noah nodded. "The men are in place. The target is the archduke. There are seven volunteers. Apis, their leader, had changed his mind and has tried to recall but they are in place and cannot be stopped. The Black Hand are disbanding and going into hiding."

"You realize this will result in war? Are you certain they cannot be recalled?" Greyson looked stunned.

"There is no way to get them word in Bosnia."

"Where will you go?" asked Noah.

"I am safe in Ireland." replied the operative. "I might head back to Mother Russia. Right now, Wilhelm is arguing with his nephew and things are not as safe there. It may be while before I see home again."

"We will do what we can," said Noah. "You have helped us much."

"Telegraph has been monitored and shut down in much of the Bosnian border." He replied as he nodded.

"When is the attack to happen?" asked Greyson.

"The first attack is a bomb. If that does not work, the other volunteers will be using various means starting June 28. One will succeed," replied the spy, lighting a small cigar.

"God speed. Be careful."

"Thank you, Noah. Safe travels."

"And to you." They all turned and left.

"Less than a week. How do we stop this?" asked Greyson.

"We can't. There is nothing we can do except follow orders and go to our next visit."

"What is that professor going to do?" asked Stephen.

"He has his hand on the scientific people in England. He can let us know if anything odd starts happening in this war that we need be concerned with," replied Greyson.

"As in Tesla odd?" asked Stephen.

Noah nodded. They got into the motorcar and headed to the dock.

At the docks, they gave their car to a gentleman from the embassy who was waiting for them. They went up the ramp, checked their tickets and joined Esther and her maid who were waiting on the deck for them.

"I'm glad to see you. The boat leaves in less than two hours." said his wife as she touched his arm.

"We know. They're pulling up the gangplank and battening hatches. They'd like to be well away before dawn." answered Noah.

"Our staterooms are close by."

"Let's go to ours and discuss events and read our orders. Then it would be good to get some sleep."

" I heard this ship is wicked fast." said Stephen.

"I understand it made the trip across in under six days. We ought to land at Sandy Hook by Sunday; taking rail from there home. Then we're staying until the baby is born. I don't give a hoot what the President says. You are not traveling until that child talks."

"Or at least cries," smiled his wife. With all this talk of war, we might not have the luxury of staying home."

Chapter 13

By the time Noah made it home, the newspapers were full of the assassination of Archduke Franz Ferdinand on June 28, 1914 by a young Serbian nationalist named Gavrilo Princip. Franz was heir to the throne of the Austro-Hungarian Empire, in Sarajevo, Bosnia. Within a month Europe was at war. In 1917, the ship that Noah had taken home was bombed and sank, killing 128 Americans and the U.S. entered the war in 1917.

The child born to Esther was a little boy named Michael David Mathias.

Adam, working in his laboratory in Atlanta, sorted through the plans they'd received from Tesla. In 1918, his father, Garrette and Gordon paid him a visit.

"Looks like there won't be a family reunion in California in 1920. Gas is rationed, and everything is short due to the war. Greyson writes from Germany that the gas masks are inadequate. We need something to drive back the Kaiser and his minions."

"I may have it," replied Adam. "I broke the code on Tesla's device, as you recall. It wasn't musk he was working with; he was using fireballs, concentrated energy to blow things up. I don't think it's capable of being commercialized. I think the reason we haven't seen it used is that whenever it's shot, the amount of energy it needs simply blows all the components. You get one shot. It's not cost effective. I think Nikolai knew that."

"That's too bad."

"I was able to redesign our gas masks: I sent a box of those to Greyson. Have we had word from Jerome?"

"He's behind enemy lines."

"Then God help him. How is his family?"

"They're brave. Helen is doing work at Red Cross and part time as a clerk to help the effort."

"So to what do I owe this visit?"

"We have a little job that's going to take some expertise."

"Really?"

"I thought the weather things and such had sort of died down in the last few months since The US joined the effort."

"Worry is that they're aiming at something bigger." said Gordon. "Besides, we think we've figured out who the mastermind was behind the break-in's at Tesla's lab and the weird occurrences. We need to put the fear of the Good Lord in a few people."

"Honestly?"

"Yes, and tonight, you, Da and I are going to go on a little excursion. It appears from our intel that the men who broke into Tesla's shop three times, who tried to use his designs are all stationed less than eight miles from Atlanta on a farm. We'll have back up from the Marshall's office."

"When do we leave?"

"I think about noon. We'll need to take the aeroplane."
"It's a two seater. We have three people?"

"Not yours. Mine," remarked Garrette. "I landed it on the field. You're going to like it."

"I can't wait. Shall I tell Lillian Rose?"

"Your wife's not really used to the Firm yet. Just tell her we're testing a new plane. She can even watch us take off."

"She might want a ride?"

"After we get back, we can do that. I've already got the gear on the plane we'll need."

"Then let's go in and tell the wife we've three extra for lunch and then get on our way."

"Sounds sensible. We'll brief you on board."

"This plane is quiet enough for that?"

"Yes, it is."

Lillian was a little flustered at the company, but she liked her father-in-law Garrette and didn't know his brother well enough to be concerned. The lunch was delightful.

"By the way, Da?" said Adam, looking at wife who blushed and nodded. "Can you pass the word to mom she's about to be a Grandma again? By our reckoning, about Christmas."

Garrette jumped up and hugged Lillian. "My dear! That's marvelous news! I fully expect Mother to dash right here when she learns about this."

"Oh, not yet. I'm just getting over the morning sickness part of this event. Maybe a little later when I'm a mite bit stronger?"

"Well, I know she'll want to send out one of the servants to help you. They can do all the hard work and you won't overtax yourself. So this is to be a Christmas surprise?"

In the meantime, Gordon was shaking his brother's hand and clapping him on the back in congratulations.

"Well," said Garrette sitting down, "We have an experiment to run with your husband for a few hours. We'll have him back around diner or a bit after, not to worry. We have a new aeroplane and we want him to help us check out its' fuel. I'd take you up but I suspect air sickness might be a little overwhelming in your condition. However, we're going to fly from this field to the airport near the Chicago munitions, fuel back up and come back. That ought to be enough of a test for the government."

"Is there any danger."

"My dear, this is surely not going to be that dangerous. There's always risk but we flew this plane here from Virginia with no problem. And the tank is still over half full. There's plenty of places to set down if we need to do so. By my reckoning, if we leave by 1, it's three hours to Chicago, and fuel up, make the report to the general, who is waiting in Chicago, and then turn around and come back. So let's see, I think eight o'clock ought to do it."

She looked at the three men. "All right. You be very careful. I want my baby to have a father when he comes into the world."

"Lilian is sure it's a son."

"Girl or boy, is no matter to us. Violet is going to pop when I tell her this tonight."

"Are you going to try to fly back to Virginia as well?"

"No, we haven't got good enough night vision to fly nights yet," remarked Gordon. "Although I do believe they're working on that."

They all left the table, Lillian included and went to see the new aeroplane.

Sitting next to the plane shed where Adam's remade Spad-VIII was tethered.

"That's huge! It's metal?" asked Garrette.

"Absolutely. It carries up to five men, pilot, copilot, bombardier, five hundred equipment to weigh it the same. Payload is a thousand pounds. The projected distance between fueling is 800 miles. Top speed is 150. At least so far. We were sort of babying her on the way down."

"How much do you project?"

"I think topping out will be 175. I don't think we're going to get them into production before the war ends. Does not mean the family can't use them."

"You have faith the War is ending soon?" Lillian asked with a hopeful tone to her voice.

74

"I think from reports that's an increasing possibility. Our boys are doing a grand job. But now let's suit up and get started."

"Suit up?" asked his brother.

"We've got these new contraptions called parachutes."

"I've heard of them."

"So if we jump from 10,000 feet, I want to live to see that grandbaby."

Lillian gasped. "Jump out? You are joking?"

"Yes, ma'am. Don't worry yourself. There, that strap goes there, this one here. If we would have to abandon ship, which is do not foresee, we get clear of the plane and pull this. You float to the ground. It makes this whole thing so much safer."

"Somehow that does not comfort me," remarked Lillian.

"We'll see you before bedtime, dear.: smiled Adam, kissing her cheek. " I don't' suppose you could get the guest rooms ready just in case we come back too late for them to fly home?"

"Of course. I can open the windows and have it all ready. I'll make soup and you can have a light supper. Love you, darling."

"And I you, dearest," smiled Adam as he touched his wife's cheek.

He climbed into the aeroplane with the others already in place and strapped himself in. He waved at his wife as he shut the door and the engine started, they began to taxi to the end of the roadway, and turned. Lillian moved back from the strip, and accelerating quickly, the big bird roared by her, nearly blowing her over in its wake, and leaped up into the air, tilted its' wings just a little and ripped open the sky as it headed up. Lillian sighed and headed back to the house. "Men, I shall never understand why they simply don't keep their feet on the ground. But there's bread to bake up, soup to put on, and I am going to get the guest rooms ready. I better check and be sure Adam shut off everything in the lab before he left. I'd hate to have something blow up while he was gone."

She walked over to the lab, saw it all seemed fine and was joined by her Labrador retriever.

"Hello, Duchess. Master's not here. Want to come up to the house for a drink, girl?"

With her hand resting on the dog's head, they walked up the paving stones to the back porch and entered. With a start, she saw there was a letter left on her kitchen table. She filled the dog's water dish, then opened the card. It read, "Tell Adam he isn't to get involved with his father's business. Bad things happen to spies."

She looked over the envelop and the note, but found no other marks. She went over to the sink and washed her hands.

"They must have left it while we were out in the field. Duchess, you feel like going through the house with me?"

Just then there was a knock on the back door. Lilian walked over.

"Good evening, sheriff. How odd you should come out tonight."

"Is Adam home? We have a problem in town we thought he might help us with."

"No, but something strange just happened. Come in, please."

She showed him the card. "It just appeared on the table while Adam and I were outdoors."

"Have you checked the rest of the house?"

"No, I just returned. Adam went with his father and brother just now on a government mission. I don't know what to think."

The Sheriff looked concerned.

"Mrs. Oberllyn, may I check your house out? I'd like to be sure there isn't anyone still here."

"I would greatly appreciate it. I don't feel quite safe right now."

"I wouldn't think so."

Nodding, he left the kitchen and checked the pantry and boot room, and the hallway, the bath and the living area and the front parlor. She joined him as he went upstairs and entered each of the bedrooms.

"Wait! Things have been rearranged here. Oh!" she gasped.

In the new baby bed, in the new nursery, a slaughtered puppy lay on the mattress. She turned away. "I'll just go get a towel to wrap the poor little thing in," she said. The sheriff grimaced.

"Mrs. Oberllyn, is there somewhere safe you can go to just until your husband returns? Don't worry about this mess. We'll fix it." He pulled out the baby sheet and rolled the puppy's body up in it.

"Perhaps the church? Perhaps we can go to the pastorate? I'm good friends with Mrs. Bruens, the pastor's wife."

"You get a few things and let's get you into town. I'll contact the boys and we'll come out and stay until Adam returns."

Chapter 14

Once at cruising altitude, around 8,000 feet, Adam opened up the engines and they all watched as the speedometer passed 125, 130, 145, 160, 165, 170 and seemed to top out at 175. He flew her that speed for an hour and backed her down.

"More tests needed but those new improvements you made to that engine are superb, Gordon. Mark that down as test of speed three on that chart over there."

"Liking it myself, " Gordon grinned back. "I'll be thinking this lady is going to make a grand bomber."

"Got to work out the delivery system. Need lots of practice on setting targets and getting within a few feet of them."

Adam hit Gordon on the shoulder. "Knew all that time you spent tearing up things as a child would come in handy someday. Now what's the plan for tonight, Da?"

"It appears that the plans that were taken from Tesla were stolen specifically for sale. The original thieves did not do anything but sell them. One went, oddly enough, to Thom, who vehemently denied it, but grudgingly agreed he had come by some of them somehow from some vague person but couldn't make hide nor hair out of all those sketches and gobbled-gook. He's been warned quietly top leave Nikolai alone. And we made him return them. He wasn't too pleased but he wants to keep his energy contracts with the Defense department. The other plans, the ones that made the death ray and the weather machine? Those went to an underground cell of the Black Hand. They experimented for a while but once their leaders were caught, tried and disposed of in Europe, they disbanded. However, two gentlemen have been putting out feelers for buyers of 'proven devices to change the weather' and such. We've researched. They were members of the Black Hand, they would have had access and now they're trying to get back money for either themselves or compatriots in Europe. They have a place south of Chicago."

"So no General?"

"One of them calls himself a general." His Father replied.

"Not our General though? I don't like to mislead the wife," frowned Adam.

"We have a cover and we are meeting with our own military. We're landing in a field near Chicago and being met by the US Marshall. They're bringing us transport the rest of the way in."

"What exactly are we going to do?"

"We recover the plans, give the spies over to the Marshall, hop back in the plane, which will have been fueled back up and head for home. It ought to be easy enough," said his brother.

"None of this is ever easy. What's the catch?" Adam said in a not too sure of this voice. "I mean, I usually am in the lab, not running about surreptiously in the night."

"We may have to disassemble a couple machines and take them home with us for you to decipher. The US Marshall may want to keep them for evidence. I don't know how large the machines are. Might maybe be too large for us to fly, in which case one of us has to arrange for ground transport and bring them home that way."

"Hence the straps in back?"

"Yes, hope the devices aren't too heavy. I'd like to get them back to your lab tonight. At any rate, we will prove out this plane on this trip. We fly from Chicago over to Washington, check in there with the military, give them the specs and fly home."

"What if they commandeer the plane?" asked Gordon.

"It blows up." answered his Father.

"Excuse me?"

"It's private property; it is also fixed to blow in case they try that. We don't want some of what we've discovered being used without proper supervision. But they can see it. That can take photos if they like. They cannot take it. They may need dissuaded."

"This is our US government?"

"And yes, it is. However, like great Grandpa used to say, 'Of course we trust our government. Just look how well that has worked for us so far...Wounded knee, Buffalo Creek, Cypress Gap...'"

"I get it. OK."

"We're meeting Teddy Roosevelt. He can be pushy,, don't let him fool you," said Father.

"What?"

"He's our contact."

"I thought he and the President didn't see eye to eye..."

"Yes, I know. But in the background, there's some other things going on. Their politics may differ but they both want passionately to finish this war and protect our country. So Teddy, besides being a bit loud at times, has sent all his boys into battle. You heard about Quentin?"

"I felt badly about him losing his boy."

"Now Teddy is really determined nothing is going to stop us winning this infernal war. So he is going to be there to meet us, as well as a few others."

"I should've dressed better."

"No need. We have blacks to wear."

"It's not dark."

"It will be where we're headed. We'll arrive in about another half hour, you two go change and get your gear together-Gordon, show him. I'll switch with Adam so I can

81

change when you're done. This plane lands in half the space of the others."

"This would make a grand bomber." Garrette finally said.

"That it would. It's not in production nor is it ready to be and as far as I'm concerned, this is a cargo carrier."

Gordon and Adam quickly changed into black clothing and put makeup on darkening their skin. Both had rifles. Both had handguns they tucked into side holsters. Both had some other devices that the firm had developed for just in case situations. Garette changed with Adam and went back himself to prepare.

Chapter 15

Lillian went to prayer meeting as was her habit and stayed that evening with the Sheriff's wife. At supper, the sheriff spoke.

"Good roast, dear. Have some more green beans, Lillian?"

"No, sir. " she smiled. "I'm afraid the little one doesn't allow me the room inside to do justice to a meal this marvelous."

Martha, the sheriff's wife asked, "Did you locate the person who got into the house, John?"

He took a deep breath. "No, but we found notes here and there. Whoever it was worked fast. You said you and the men weren't out in the field more than half an hour or so?"

"That's what it seemed like."

"Well, we found five notes, all over the house. They must have been watching. They must have seen all the men leave and they snuck in then. Funny the dog didn't bark."

"Duchess is usually a good watchdog. I don't understand it either. She was near us by the plane and perhaps didn't hear the stranger when the plane was lifting off?"

"I don't know. The person was obviously trying to frighten you good."

"Well, they more than succeeded."

"You said Adam was due back tonight?"

"Yes, he and his father and brother were testing something for the war effort. I can't say much more than that since I really don't understand most of it. They do it quite often. He has a defense contract."

"I understand," said the sheriff. "Well, I've left two deputies on the property to watch it til he comes home. In the meantime, you need to get some rest. I've not delivered a baby in a long time and I have no intention of doing it now."

Lillian was shown to the guest room where she lie down for what seemed like hours, unable to rest, waiting to hear the roar of a plane going over that would tell her Adam was on his way home. She fell asleep hearing nothing but the sound of spring frogs and crickets.

Chapter 16

In the pre-light over the meadows, Grayson waited with his platoon. He'd deli levered his message from Pershing and now it was a matter of waiting for the inevitable fight to start. *At least I'm using that French mom used to try and pound into my brain. Couldn't see much use for it then, but she was right. Wonder when I'll see home again? Hope I can get that letter out to Cora May tomorrow. Got it all written but haven't been able to get it to her. Hope that baby Timothy is over the colicky stage. Wish I could have seen him before I came over here. She says he's a sweet little guy, takes over Grandpa Noah. Oh, Lord, here they come! Be with me, Father. This is going to be a long day. Wish I'd never heard of the Hindenburg line.*

They fought for days, reacting, responding to the Germans, back and forth up the canal at Somme. By the time it was done, over eleven thousand Americans had lost their lives. Greyson considered himself lucky to have escaped without injury. He reported back to his commanding officer and was sent with a message to Commander Foch of the French army, who sent him back with another message.

"It appears radio communications aren't working well, sir," he said apologetically. "This letter is from their command."

"Risking lives to send notes," fumed the Commander. he got up and went over to the map. "We're here. No more messages. I'm sending our unit here and here. Pershing wants a major offensive just with US men. The French are dilly dallying. Oh, and you have a new assignment. Oberllyn, your division is being sent to Belleau Wood. Hope it's quieter for you there than here. They need scouts. You're the best we've got. You take care of yourself, son."

Loading up in a troop carrier, Greyson stole a look at the picture of his wife he carried in his metal encase new testament as he rumbled along with the other men. Putting it away, he spoke to the man next to him.

"Don't believe I've had the pleasure?" he said politely.

"Tisn't any pleasure here, mate," answered the other man. "Names Robert. That your Sheila?"

"Mt? Oh, yes, that was a picture of my wife. Are you married?"

The man nodded. "Yes. My wife is home with our son Malcom and daughter Mary. Sweet little things they are. They're hoping their Da comes back soon. Hope to be home by Christmas, if they don't gas us again."

"You must be from Australia?"

"Naw, New Zealand. Close enough though."

"You been gassed?"

"Who hasn't? My mask got tore in the last battle though and I found some tape but they got no replacements. Not looking forward to battle without one."

"Tell you what," said Greyson. "Let me help with that. My brother's a scientist. He sent me some gas masks, little different, but they work. I have an extra one. Here, let me show you how it works."

He got into his pack and hauled out the mask."

"It's lighter. You sure it works?"

"Got me through the last battle. Let's get it adjusted to you." After some finagling with straps, the mask fit almost perfectly. They took it off and he stowed it away with his gear. They rode on, jerking and bumping, shifting side to side until late that evening, telling stories of home, getting

. acquainted as men do when faced with death. They arrived at the next camp. They went to their assigned shelter and listened to the far off sound of gunfire.

The next morning, Greyson woke early, said a prayer, ate some k rations cold. He checked his gun and checked on his friend. Their new commander came by.

"Men, we're going to be leaving these woods after tomorrow. Until then, we have to get to the target, take it and get out. Word is the gas is going to be really thick. Put your masks on and don't leave them off. We're going to take hill number 142 and its going to be bad. Keep your heads down. Follow the man in front of you and be careful. God be with us all."

As the marines advanced, Smoke and gas drifted by them. The noise became unbearable; Greyson was running out of ammunition. As he came up behind some trees and over a rise, he saw a trench in front of him, with a machine gun mowing down his friends and fellow marines. They were pinned down by the bullets. He motioned to Malcom and the others to don their masks, and motioned towards the trench. He rolled closer, opened fire, shot his last bullets, and jumped into the trench with just his bayonet. His last thought was of his wife and the son he would never meet.

Robert saw, and in the lull as the Germans were murdering his friend, gave a sign to his comrades and they went in after Greyson, taking out the Germans and the guns. Later that day, the capture of hill 142 would be complete. The telegram home arrived a week later. Cora May took her son and moved back to Colorado to be near her folks.

That night, Robert opened his flask, took a swig and held it up to the sky. "If there's a God, may he let me avenge the man who's kindness saved me from the gas today and who's courage saved the unit from certain death. I'll send that letter to his wife, and let her know he is being buried here in

France. My son Malcom will know of this man and his family, and someday, maybe we can repay him for his kindness."

Chapter 17

Adam, Garrette and Gordon rode in silence towards their objective. A mile away, they got out and slipped through the trees at the edge of town, to the warehouses nearby.

It was dark and cool inside the warehouse. They stayed to the edges, watching, looking and listening. Finally Garrette pointed with his chin.

Two men were seated by a table. Beside them was a flat satchel, next to them a large crate.

They sat still, backs to the Oberllyns. Garrette stopped, held up his hand and watched. Then men did not move. He motioned the others back into the dark edges of the building.

He held up his hand and began using sign language.

"I think they're dead or drugged," he signed. "We need to find out. The box may not be what it is supposed to be."

Gordon nodded. "I can find out. I go up and look." He motioned towards a ladder. Garrette shook his head.

"They would expect you to try that. Follow me."

They circled in the almost dark, against the walls, around shelving, behind boxes watching. The men never moved. At another vantage point, Adam pointed out and signed "Wire taped table leg-attached to box." Garrette nodded. He took something out of his pocket. He tossed it close to the men's chairs-the percussive popper snapped and let out some smoke and they never moved.

He signed "dead-that close, even drugged would respond. It's a trap. Out."

As they turned to go, there was growl. In the dark, out of a side room bounded two Rottweiler dogs. Gordon made a small sound , a buzz in his throat. He pulled a whistle out of his pocket and blew it-making nothing but high frequency noises. The dogs stopped in their tracks, tilting their heads, confused. He blew again and they started to back up, finally turning and running back to the room. There were noises inside. Gordon motioned to the others and they went quickly to the sides of the door. Gordon pulled out his revolver and stepped inside, at the ready.

Two men were tied to a chair, but much alive, gagged. They shook their heads violently as they tried to warn Gordon.

Under the table was another box, also rigged to blow. Adam stood outside the door, keeping watch. Garette entered the room, took a look, then motioned for Adam.

"You think we can disarm it?"

"Looks like a pretty simple design. You think these are our contacts?"

"You boys supposed to be meeting buyers?"

The men nodded. Gordon checked their bonds, then took off the gags.

"We thought you'd come earlier. Three men came, with a briefcase of money and then suddenly five more came in," babbled one of them Two of your people got shot and they took them out there, tied us up here. They didn't even take anything, I don't think. The box with the device is under this table."

"What's the box out there?"

"I don't know. The actual device is in the box under here."

"The schematics?"

"They're in a small brown satchel."

"So the satchel is rigged to blow out there and the box is rigged to blow in here," mused Garrette. "what do you think Da?"

"Gordon, you step outside the door and keep watch. I'll get this one disarmed and we can open it, see what's inside, i

90

it's what we want. We'll worry about that satchel after. We can re-engineer backwards if this is a working prototype."

"It is working." said the other man. "I built it and I changed the weather over the plains last winter. Did you notice the flooding and the snowstorms at odd times and odd places? That was me."

"No, that was a stolen plan you got from Nikolai. You're just a technician."

"Tesla's plans did not work. I built them. I had to re-engineer enough of it that it's nothing like his plans. It's my design."

"I don't think so." Adam stood up and shoved the box out from under the table. "It's pretty heavy. Let me check it over."

"Disarmed?"

"One bomb is. I don't know what else is coming."

"I did not put a trap in the box," blustered captive number 1. "I would not blow up my machine."

Adam checked it, took a small chisel out of his pocket and lifted the lid from the crate. Inside, packed in excelsior, was a device neatly and securely settled in. He studied it a moment.

"This look like it's all here?" He asked the captives.

The man leaned forward. Adam shoved the table out of the way so he could see. "It hasn't been touched. It won't run without the key."

"And you have the key?"

"And when I am paid, you will have the key."

"Is the key here or do we need to go on one of these long wild goose chases to get it?" asked Garrette.

"I have the key here." The dogs growled. Gordon blew his whistle and they settled. He tilted his head and then left the door to go over to the two dogs. Gently patting them, he removed their collars. There was a key taped inside each collar.

"Might these be useful?" he asked Adam.

"Looks like a double blind system. He gives us this key, that one is the real one-see very similar but has a chip out of it. Clever. We'd pay them off and it still would not work."

The captive blustered. "Those are not the keys. I have the keys."

"You said key before," said Adam mildly.

Gordon brought over a dolly and they loaded up the box. "Let's go! Those killers might come back."

"True, they might, whomever they were." replied Garrette. "But they're killers and you're terrorists. I don't know that I can trust either of you. At least over there on that side table is a pocket knife. You can get yourselves out of this in a few minutes. In the meantime, your two friends are booby trapped to what seems like a brown satchel and another box in the middle of the next room. Any idea what's in that box?'

"I don't know," said captive two. "They said something about blowing the warehouse and everything in it when they left, but they didn't take the device or the designs or anything that I could see. They just set those boxes over there."

"Gordon," began Garrette.

"On it." He went back to the large room and circled closer to the middle, a step, pause, step, pause as he searched high, low, for cameras or trip wires, anything that could be not easily seen.

He got closer, tilted his head, nodded, studied and came back.

"Box is marked dynamite. There's a wire from the satchel to the box, and it appears to have a timer on it. It says 4:45."

"I am guessing in fifteen minutes this place is going to blow and that if we pick up the satchel, it triggers as well."

"Men are bled out."

One of the captives was crying. "One of those boys was my son and that's his best friend. They did not deserve to die."

92

"Nor do all the people that are in this area. That's enough to start a major explosion and the fires after could wipe out the warehouse district. Everyone's at home this time of night and the causalities will be high."

"We've got to disarm it, Da," said Gordon. "There are three trip wires. There's a wire to the bag. There's a wire attached to the box. All the wires appear to be the same color."

"Really? Hard to believe folks would not adhere to national codes." smiled Adam. "You think you can disarm it? I'll leave this right here. Da, maybe you put the pocket knife a little higher til we're done so we don't have any interference."

"I got a better idea," said Pa. "There's another dolly. Let's take them outside the building in case it blows, they can be a little safer, and we can have peace."

"I think, Da, leaving them here is fine." said Adam. "I just got this hunch."

"Really?" Da raised his eyebrow.

"Yeah. Come on Gordon."

Adam headed across the floor, with a very odd look on his face, wire cutter in his hands. He got to the table, reached over and poked one of the men. He shook his head. Gordon studied him quizzically. Adam took the pry bar from Gordon and went under the table, studying the crate. He put the pry bar on it.

"Wait, Adam! I am not going to be blown to kingdom come..."

"No, you aren't. You notice the word dynamite is spelled wrong? Box looks empty. There's a paper in the bottom." He reached in, pulled it out. Then he took a sharp knife from his pocket, held the satchel carefully down and cut it open. It contained blank papers.

"I don't get it."

"You will. Where's Da?"

"Right here," said Garrette. "What's going on?"

93

"We head for home now. This was a ruse. They're going to hit the labs and they wanted us away."

They left far more quickly than they came.

"The timer was dead, there was no explosives and those men in the chair were wax figures. The machine in the box was a simple ozone generator that Tesla was selling twenty years ago. It could no more influence the weather than I can. If we waited around, I bet 4:45 is when the local police have been told to come bust some terrorists and we'd be tied up for hours breaking through the red tape."

They walked quickly towards the car, then broke into a run around the corner, trotting together, hats off, as the local police roared by towards the warehouse district. They arrived at their car and Garrette stopped them.

"Hold on. That wire was not there before."

"You're right," said Gordon. "It goes into the gas tank, under the frame, in the bottom of the door, and to the gas pedal."

"They were taking care of us this way if the other deterrent didn't take long enough. They figured if we were in a hurry to leave, we'd jump in, and blow ourselves up. What do you guess someone's waiting to see if this blows?"

"Most likely. Parked where we are, it's not really going to harm much. Let her blow."

"Da, it's a fifteen minute drive but a three hour walk back to the airport. We blow the car?"

"I know someone. Garrette had opened the door and tied a string to the wire.

"Step over here, guys. What did the note say?" Adam handed it over to him. Da turned it over. On the sheet were written the word, "Gotcha."

"Yep, we been had. I'll bet Teddy knows nothing about seeing us."

"Who do you think the mole is?" Garrette pulled the string. There was a click and the gas tank exploded beautifully.

"I'd say we'd had a hard time surviving that," remarked Da. "Looks pretty thorough."

"Yeah and my guess is those guys back there have some cock and bull story about us to tell the police, who are going to waste good taxpayer dollars trying to find out why the Oberllyns would be here to attack and tie up good citizens in warehouses."

"I can run interference with that, but how do we get back to the plane?" asked Adam.

"Let's wait a few minutes and see if anybody comes. You want to join me in that pub over there?"

"Haven't had a good cold birch beer in a few days," answered Gordon. They walked down a block and entered the tavern, where they ordered soft drinks and waited by the window. Most of the patrons had run out at the sound of the explosion. The fire truck roared in a few moments later and they watched.

They completed their sodas and came back out, then walked quietly down the street, turned a corner and up another. In a few moments they had come to a quiet side street. Garrette knocked at the door and a lady came to it.

"Garrette Oberllyn, what are you doing hereabouts? And you boys have grown. Well, don't just stand there, get in here." They entered the small house.

"Sorry to bother you, Edith but we really need to get to the airport."

"You into those noisy things now? And were you maybe near that boom I just heard?"

"Yepper, that was the automobile."

"Never did like them things. Here, you hold the baby. Steve! Go harness up Macky and Sam."

95

She went over to the closet. "Now get those black things off, here, you put this vest on, and you put this light jacket on and you, lordy what a mop of hair you've got!"

Adam smiled sheepishly. "I been meaning to get a haircut."

"Yes, indeed. You married, son?"

"Yes, ma'am."

"Then' I'll leave it up to her to take you in line. Here, put this cap on over it and change the black shirt to this nice blue one. There, that ought to help. Now, you hold Sally, and you take the baby, Garrette, don't know as to how you other boys have had any experiences with babies. Let's go." She put on a bonnet and shawl and led them out to the back where she had an old fashioned wagon set up. "Gordon, you drive. I'll set up here with the baby, you boys in back with Sally, and we'll just look as if we're out for a drive. Not running away or anything. Steve, hold down the fort and don't let the beans burn. If I'm not back by when the bread's raised, put it in the oven."

"I can't go, Ma?"

"Sorry, son. Don't need you getting any ideas from these fellows." Gordon clicked his tongue and the buggy horses started out into the street, first at a fast walk, then a canter. They stopped at corners, then trotted on. Once they left the small town suburbs, he put the horses to a run and kept it that was for the first mile or so, then back to a trot and then canter and back up. In a short time, the airport came into view.

"Now, Gordon, don't you worry none about us getting back. Happy to give you a ride and I'll not be asking about what's going on cause I know you can't tell me. But you say hello to the Genevieve for me. Haven't had a good talk with her in ages."

"You need to bring the children and visit before snow flies. The farm's lovely."

"I know it is. You wouldn't happen to know of any land around you for sale? I need to get my young'un's out of the city. Now that my man's gone, I got no need to stay here for his job. I've got a little laid by, and I was thinking moving out to the country might suit us well."

"I might know a place," said Adam as they drew up. "There's a small place near ours that just came up. House, barn, ten acres, about half woods. Has a good well, and a stream. I don't know what they're asking for it but the natives are friendly."

"I think I know the place," remarked Garrette. "Old man Franks lived there. Hasn't it been empty for a few months?"

"Yes, it has. It needs paint but I don't think the town's asking much for it. He hadn't any relatives so they've got the deed at town hall. I could make some inquiries about it if you'd like." They pulled up to the airport.

"I'd appreciate that. Been getting crowded and last week had a visit from some odd people asking about your family and what did I know about you. I told them my Danny had worked with you, but that I really didn't even know where you were right now. I suspected you still worked for the government but it wasn't my place to worry about your family when I had my own to worry about. I got widows' benefits, for sure, but we aren't exactly rolling in the wealth. I chattered them out of the house and they eventually gave it up. Oh, they tried the threats routine and I told them off and tossed them out on their ears. Then later that week, one of the regulars from the tavern came by and 'accidentally' dropped his bottle in my yard and dropped a cigar into it when he stumbled. Little Steve was there and put it out fast, but it's sort of a wakeup call that I ought to cooperate. I called the number you gave me and made a report and no one else has come around. Still, I'm thinking it's time for a change."

"Tell you what." said Garrette. "You go ahead and pack up everything. I'll send some guys and we can bring you out to a safer place. It's evident they aren't going to stop harassing folks. This is Tuesday-can you be packed up by Thursday? I'll send a wagon by."

"That's mighty kind of you, I didn't mean to cause any problems."

"You've done so much, and with Danny gone, I feel it's our duty. We'll make arrangements and I'll send one of my boys to get you. He'll have the other half of this coin with him." He handed her a half dollar which had been cut in half, leaving a jagged edge. "It's a couple day trip there, but you'll be fine."

"Thank you, Garrette."

"Thank you for the ride. Let's see if those fellas actually protected the plane."

The men climbed down. They handed the extra clothes back to Edith and she turned the buggy and trotted back. The Oberllyn's walked the last few steps to the hanger and went inside.

The soldiers that were on duty saluted. Garrette and Adam walked around the plane.

"She appears fine, Garrette," said Gordon.

"Do you have your package, sir?" asked one of the men.

"We have what we came for," answered Garrette, looking at the men carefully. "Anything happen here at the hanger?"

"No sir. It's all been quiet."

Adam was in the cockpit, poking around. "Nothing seems changed. And that's odd." he said softly to Gordon.

"Oh?"

"I left a list of things to be done with the bird while I was gone. They haven't been done. And those are not the two guards we left." Gordon nodded. He carefully looked from the vantage of the cockpit and pointed with his chin. The side door to the hanger was open.

"It safe to fly?"

"She's not bulletproof."

"Fraid of that. We need to take the fight outside."

"We also need to protect our helper who is trotting back to town alone with two small kids and vulnerable to attack."

"And Da's out there talking to the fake soldier."

"I suspect the next few minutes are going to be interesting."

"Yep. Got a prayer handy?"

"and a couple guns. Lord, be with us now and help us to be safe and God bless the US of A." They climbed out of the plane.

"She seems fine, Garrette," Adam said loudly. "I'd like to back her out back to fuel her and be sure. . Tanks on the left side of the hanger. You guys stand clear."

"Fine, you make your tests and fill her up. It is an experimental aeroplane, so you be careful."

He turned back to the guard. "Best back up a bit, the prop wash is pretty bad on this plane. Got a little more power than most."

"Really? Is this the new cargo plane for the war effort?"

"No, that's in Virginia. Over here would be good. Yes, just fine."

Gordon stepped the other way, with his hands in his pockets. The plane started up and Gordon helped direct the backing up process.

"Where is the package we're supposed to help load? I didn't see you bring anything in," started the guard. He bent over as Garrette mashed his fist into his midsection and followed it up with a closed fist to his neck. As he hit the floor, eight men started to run into the hanger from behind boxes stacked here and there, but Gordon tossed a small metal cylinder that blew up in their faces, leaving them coughing and collapsing on the floor.

He ran to join Garrette as they ran out to the field, then over to Adam. Adam had pulled the plane over to the tanks and was filling it up.

"I'll put in whatever I can in the next minute but it won't be full. Those guys dissuaded?"

"Don't know. Any idea where the real guys went?"

"Two men appear to be trussed up over there."

"My guess is those are our guys. Let's see if we can load them up. You fuel, Gordon, come on. They don't need any more abuse. We'll load them and head for the next base. We have enough fuel to reach the destination?"

"You don't honestly think Teddy is going to show?"

"No, but I think it would be a good thing to make a phone call and the lines are cut here."

"Yeah." Adam turned to fueling as Garrette and Gordon ran over, pulled the stunned guards to their feet, and pulled them back to the plane. They yanked them inside, checked the dog tags around their neck and nodded. A quick check showed no weaponry. One of them groaned.

Adam closed off the fuel, being sure there could be no spark as he took off, then got in.

Gordon was in the pilot seat; he started the aeroplane and back it toward the field. In the back they could see a couple men stagger out of the hanger with weapons, still coughing. They heard guns firing but none seemed to come near the plane.

"Head for the base. It's closest." The plane banked, headed west.

The soldiers were coming to. Garrette let them wake up, and then spoke.

"Fellas, sorry for the noise. It's hard to hear in the plane. That's some goose egg you got there, son. Now just stay still while I get you cut free. Steady now. There. You ready? Ok, there, rub your arms to get some feeling back in them."

"Last thing I remember some guy with a rock in a sock type thing slugged Jim and then I had a noose around my neck and now I'm in a plane?"

"Yeah. You got knocked out. We'll drop you off in New York. I can phone your regiment from there and explain what happened."

"I can't understand you very well. Who attacked us?"

"I wish I knew but they didn't damage the plane, they didn't steal it, and we'll all be fine. Rest back and your commanding officer can debrief you. Right now, just lie back. We're about an hour or so by air."

Landing in a private field a little later, Garrette went in and made a couple calls at the office. In a short time an army jeep showed up, collected the soldiers and left. Garrette had written out a letter to their commander. Adam had filled the tank full and they'd gone over it carefully. Finding nothing, they got more worried.

"First Greyson dies in a battle he wasn't supposed to be anywhere near. Now it appears the labs are under attack. I've called your Mother and she's battening down the hatches. I'm pretty sure they're at your place, Adam."

"What? But my wife is all alone there except for the dog."

"She is safe at the Sheriff's house. His men have circled the wagons, so to speak and are going over it. I've called in some of our folks as well."

"We've got to be more careful."

"Yes, and I've got a bad feeling the weather's going to get worse as we head south."

"Weather map shows clear."

"But whomever set up this wild goose chase does not want us to arrive. If they do have a working machine, what better thing to do than blow us out of the sky?"

"So what do you want to do?"

"We aren't flying straight home."

Chapter 18

Jerome looked at Helen and the other wives.

"Now, really ladies, we've gone long past worrying about these fake obituaries of the fake newspapers that keep showing up predicting our husbands' deaths. It was odd the first time. Now it appears we're being told Adam is going to crash his plane."

"It's getting bothersome," replied his wife.

"I'm glad Cora Mae took Timmy and went to Colorado to live away from all this mess. Greyson's death has been hard on us all." Jerome replied.

"I just wish this cursed war would stop."

"Well, the last offensive went well. Since the US has joined in, we've been beating them back."

"But at what cost? Thousands are dying."

Esther nodded. "I agree. War never makes sense."

"Is there any new information from the inventors?"

"We've disproved Tesla's weather device :it does sort of work but it's too unpredictable. It's not exact enough; you're just as soon able to get snow as rain in an area.. Maybe someone someday can make it stable. Right now Tesla's trying to make a boat disappear, sort of a hide it in plain sight device. My thought is Thom behind the papers; just to cause trouble with a rival. Adam's new plane will help move cargo. My thought is the war will soon be over. A lot of bad has come out of this war, but a lot of good as well."

"Good?"

"Oberllyns are now scattered all over the place. We've got labs in Colorado, a base in California and North Carolina, and the home base in Washington. We've built our base and have operatives quietly living abroad. Maybe, just maybe, we can help prevent the next war, or at least make it shorter."

"Yet our people live on reservations," replied Genevieve. "Our children get put in boarding schools and our people die of diseases no one else gets anymore because they don't have access to health care." Helen nodded. "I know, Mother. It's one of the reasons we've used so many of our own people as operatives. The other government agencies are starting to notice."

Later that evening, Adam landed at the home strip. Garrette and his sons greeted the sheriff and they all went over the house again. Nothing was found wrong but a newspaper was lying on the rocker. Garrette looked at it and shook his head.

"Sheriff, I wish there was some way we could trace where these come from. This purports to be a copy of the Tarkington Times. In it, we are supposed to have died earlier today landing that plane. Well, we aren't dead, and these are not our obituaries."

The sheriff took it and shook his head. "I don't know, Mr. Oberllyn, whomever your enemies are, they sure have got interesting imaginations. You mind if I take this?"

"Not at all. I suspicion they've sent copies to our homes. Wife most likely already has it."

"I can check with the local newspaper office, but this really doesn't look like the type from there. He might give me a lead though as to who does do this sort of thing."

The sheriff left. Helen went over to the radio set and turned it on.

"I wonder if radio will ever be used for something besides news bulletins and war communications," she said to no one in particular.

"We interrupt this programme to bring you good news,' the radio blared. "As of eleven o'clock today, the eleventh day of the eleventh month, the war is officially over! Armistice is here. The war, I repeat is over."

"What?"

"I heard about it a few weeks ago. However, I wasn't certain at all it would occur," replied Adam, coming over and putting his arm around her waist.. "Maybe we can just go back to being regular scientists now and not have to worry about our people."

"Maybe some of them can come home?" Garrette shook his head. "Some may, but most want to stay and try to build lives in the countries they've adopted. It's not like reservation life has a lot to offer."

"What do we do now?" mused Virginia.

"We build, we prepare. Just because the Allies are asking huge amounts of money in reparations from Germany doesn't mean they won't try this again. They're pretty crippled right now, but they're stubborn. And we still haven't got the ringleaders.

"We don't?"

"No, for one thing, we keep dying in the newspapers."

"Oh, those. They're just silly," said his wife.

"No, dear, there was a pattern. Before every large offensive, we'd get a newspaper announcing our deaths. Greyson did get killed. He was actually assigned to be two hundred miles south from that battle. The orders that sent him to the front instead of his assignment were not traceable. Someone succeeded in getting one of our people sent to the wrong place at the wrong time and we lost him."

"Many families lost sons in the war," began Genevieve.

"I know. And any life lost is tragic and so many deaths in this war were unneeded. However, the fact is there is a mole somewhere and there is someone pulling the strings behind the scenes."

"But at least all our boys come home now."

105

Garrette nodded. "Yes, we come home, but meanwhile, Europe is in tatters and so many people are displaced and hurt. And I can't help wondering about who is behind all this. Wilhelm was always somewhat of a braggart and very ambitious, but even that wouldn't have caused all this to erupt as it did without help from something else. Someone had to be backing it to get it the point of war."

"Are you turning conspiracy theorist on me, dear?' smiled his wife.

"No, just forever seeing patterns where maybe none actually exist. I'm happy for the wars' end. Maybe we can have peace now that the war to end wars is done. I don't know. Let's hope. In the meantime, we need to consolidate our holdings and spend time just doing research wherever it takes us."

"I for one, will find research alone just refreshing.' Adam said. "let's have a toast to peace, and then I'm back to the lab. Got some shakedown to do before the delivery of that bird.'

Chapter 19

Years passed, troubling years of depression and starvation for most of the world. The reservations were hard hit. Genevieve and her family sent frequent packages to the differing tribes to try and ease the burdens of the people. They increased their personal farms and hired in all they could afford to give people jobs and be able to give food away. They petitioned the government but there were so many other things that seemed more important than the plight of a few lowly aboriginal peoples on reservations. The Presidents in succession had to deal with the crash of Wall Street, the Great Depression, elections every four years and a crumbling infrastructure. There was a growing fear that Europe was going to erupt again in anger over the reparations forced on it by a world that didn't want it to grow large enough to become a threat ever again. Feeding on the fear and starvation of the people, a little known man named Adolf Hitler took the government of Germany over with promises he would make Germany great again and it would last a thousand years.

Back home, Garrette and Genevieve retired to the family home in California. Surrounded by groves of fruit and family, they enjoyed hosting the reunion every ten years. Jerome and Adam were now in charge of the family firm; Adam ran the think tanks and Jerome headed up foreign affairs. He was a master at negotiating and espionage.

Esther and her husband Noah moved to South America to set up a think tank studying ostensibly the lives of hummingbirds but sending reports back to Jerome about the varying political situations and setting up safe houses for agents. Gordon and his wife Virginia moved back to France to set up a branch of the family and head up operations. They added a son to their family in the middle of the war and named him Theodore Wild Fox; he became a tracker of no little repute in France, working closely with the official police in solving crimes after the war and building a name for the family making important connections. Several times he asked for help from back home and they always came from America. Wildfox had a gift for languages and became proficient in German, French, English, Chinese and Slavic languages. Jerome found him invaluable.

Gordon's wife Virginia helped arrange protection for several scientists caught between the Nazi regime and the war aiding them in escaping to friendlier countries. The firm interceded with the government red tape and enabled a physicist to emigrate to Princeton. Other scientists followed and formed a joint task force, and the firm acted as liaisons with the government and the men of the Manhattan Project. He'd seen enough of death. His father Garrette had passed just before the Enola gay made her flight. Adam and Jerome retired, Adam to California in 1947, and Jerome to Colorado in 1948.

The French part of the family never failed to put flowers on the mass grave where their brother Greyson was buried every Armistice day.

Adam's boy Glen moved to England, first to study at Oxford and then to run intelligence in England. He was instrumental in preventing Lord Mountbatten from being assassinated. For this he was knighted and became a member of the British empire, which earned him no end of teasing from his brothers.

The 1950 reunion was in a time of peace; America was riding high on the victory of World War 11; the economy was booming; veterans' were building homes and going to school. The world seemed at peace.

Adam's son Glen raised his glass. All the various branches of the family had sent representatives to the reunion from all over the globe.

"To all the generations before, and to those yet to come for seven generations, may this old world find peace finally." They all stood around the ancient picnic tables under the old oaks, raised their glasses and drank of the hard cider made there on the farm in the tradition of Noah Oberllyn.

"And may this family continue on, aiding peace, destroying the enemies of tranquility, and keeping the traditions alive." Another toast drank after Glen's father spoke.

Over on a large table, stretched out, pages glued together into a whole, was a time worn and venerable document stretching out under glass paperweights, eight feet wide, ten feet long. Some of the ink was faint and had been touched up a little with a steady hand so it was readable. Wildfox stood next to it with a pen in his hand. Small lines had carefully been drawn the night before where names were to be signed. The people surrounded it as the generations were read.

"These are the generations of the Family Oberllyn since they left Scotland and came back to the homeland in America," Adam began. "I read only the elder men, not to slight the women, but my good wife will read those in turn, so that all may remember the hardships, the sorrows, the joys together. Then each family head represented here will add their children to the lines, and the newly married to the family, so that this may be kept a growing and living document. In the year 1834, our Grandparents were captured by a neighboring tribe and sold into slavery to an Englishman who took them to England and sold them into indenturehood to a Scottish candlemaker. He was a good master and taught them a trade, allowed them to earn their way to freedom and since he had no children, sold his shop to them. They could not inherit due to British law, but they could buy, so they had the shop and ran it well for five years.

They had a little girl, they had a son who died of fever. The little girl was educated and shortly after, the family came back from England, naturalized Scottish citizens, bought a farm, set up their candle making business for a while, and that young woman, our first professor, married into the Oberllyn clan. They lived in Indiana. They had many children. One family, headed up by our great grandfather, distinguished himself in the military and as a detective and as a farmer and scientist. That was Noah, who had moved here to this land of California by wagon with his wife and children in 1860. Of all those children, many stayed on the farm in California, right here on this land, and became farmers and tradesman. Some left to gain more education and followed their Mother's footsteps in tradition and in education and some their father's in invention and agriculture.

However, some of the family decided to take a more studied approach towards helping the world become a safer place and they founded what we have lovingly named The Firm. We are dedicated to science and observation of world events and interceding when it seems right..." the listing of the generations and the names went on for nearly two hours, reiterating the stories of the ancestors of the family. Finally, the new members were added to the scroll. On other tables, new copies of the scroll were made to be kept in different countries with different members of the family, so the tradition would continue if something happened in one country, it would not be lost. And finally assignment of family operations was made.

"After careful discussion of abilities and likes and resources, we make the following adaptations and changes in the family structure," began Adam.

"First, I have stepped down from heading the firm and am taking over as patriarch of our assembled family. Jerome is retired also, well, as well as one with his energy retires. I am not sure the lab in Colorado is going to survive his experiments.

110

Gordon, as you know, suffered a stroke last year and has already taken his place among the sky elders watching over us. I and wife have moved into the old log cabin and will host these proceedings every ten years as long as the Creator gives us strength. My son Glen will act as coordinator and war chief of the family firm now, with Jerome's son Michael Everett, who is an attaché in Washington, as peace chief heading up our Washington post. Everett's son, Noel, has joined the military and is in training for special forces. Gordon's daughter, Angelica Summermoon, will take my post as head of laboratories. She is a brilliant young woman and well able to do this for us. The rest of the family members are in homes and on land that has been in our family for generations and are asked to continue to keep them in good order, to help those of us in active service to this country, to Turtle island, and to the family first of all. "

His brother Jerome stood up. "You know that our father Garrette always thought there was a shadow working in the background of the government; seemingly behind the start up of wars for profit and power. At any rate, they always seemed to send us newspapers about our imminent deaths. They seemed to be behind the stealing of inventions that might have helped mankind. They seemed to try and stop us when we brought over certain scientists marked for death by the Nazi regime, and who were our salvation in the war. We always seemed one step behind them. I bring you the latest that we have been able to find out. First, we have not stopped them. They are at this point agitating in another part of the world to start yet another war. This one will be in Asia. Our country will be alone in the battle for much of it. Whomever is doing this is heavily in the arms sales, but also in the human trafficking trade as well. We have settled that there are at least one arm of their group in each of the civilized countries; they are not attached to the Mafia, nor to the several wealthy families that have been accused of such in the past, the Rockefeller's, the Rothschild's, the Betancourt's. They are an independent force and seem to hold a philosophy of man being just another creature on the earth that needs to be culled. It's very disturbing. They worship nature. They're quite pagan and they are amoral. Everything is relative to them. We haven't even got a proper name, but we have traced members of their group to Parliament, to Congress, to other governments, slowly entering into the seats of government. They have to be rooted out and stopped. For some reason, they think we First Nations are special and ought to join with them and they can be quite persuasive. No matter what happens on the world scene, this is the real enemy. We only know them as Bruderschaft."

"Brotherhood??" asked Wild Fox. "So are they German based?"

"They supposedly trace themselves back to the White Brotherhood of Egypt. Hitler was obsessed with them. They have some pretty rich people and influential folks involved." replied Jerome.

"Then they bear watching closely. What's this about Asia?" asked Everett.

"Our intelligence is estimating that we will enter a war in Vietnam and the French will leave. The French have no more money or resources to spend on this, they have been drained by the conflict. We in the US are seen as a bottomless pot of supplies to these people. Ostensibly it's about democracy. We don't think so. It's pretty much all greed." There was quiet as all digested this latest information.

"One last thing. Did we ever find out who was sending all those newspaper reports?" asked Esther.

Jerome laughed. "That we did discover and stop. One of the members of this Brotherhood was disenchanted with some of the other members and tried to take things into his hands by trying to send us the obituaries as coded messages. This deceived person actually thought he was helping us with his warnings. We know that he was taken out by his own people. However, we learned much from him before they caught up with him and took him out. He was an Austrian immigrant. We are indebted to him for some of the intel he gave us. We tried to give him a safe place to hide, but he didn't want it. He was assassinated a week after speaking to us."

Angelica stood up. "Then I thank him although for years he was a thorn in our elder's sides. However, I think it's time the labs gave report of present and future projects."

The reports were given and compared, stories exchanged. Supper was served and everyone visited; some had to leave to catch trains, some went to bed to start out in the morning; but the 1950 reunion finished.

Chapter 20

"Skinwalker, you ok?" whispered Noel.

"Held down by fire, 'bout as well as can be expected, friend." He fired his gun, quickly rolled away.

Noel did the same and rolled the other way. Gunfire concentrated on where they were a few seconds earlier. In the meantime, Noel had slithered around and was by Skinwalker side again.

"We got to take out that nest," he said.

"I'd agree. How 'bout you just sort of fly over and drop a bomb?"

"Got no bombs nor wings. However, got some tricks taught me by old Storyteller. You keep me covered."

"Wait, you're going where?"

"Left-just keep up camo firing. Ready? OK, on my count, one, two, three, now." Noel rolled under bushes, then crawled as Skinwalker, Malcom's youngest son fired erratically, moved, drew fire towards himself. Noel stayed low and quiet, and circled the platoon of cong. He worked his way inward, tree to tree, bush to bush. He took a long heavy stick and a shoelace from his boot. He tied a grenade to the stick, set the end of the stick in the lace, pulled the pin and then swung the home made atlatl up and flung the stick. It landed in the midst of the platoon and blew. He hit the ground, holding his shoulder where a piece of flying metal debris had embedded itself. The cong nest went quiet.

In the ensuing silence, marines ran up and finished the cleanup of the enemy. Skinwalker joined his cousin.

"Even for a half gone boonie nut that was the craziest thing I've ever seen, son. Here, let me get a bandage on that, don't think I better pull it out. Just let me tie this. Yes. They got our medic. You'll have to contend with me."

"We still have to take the hill."

"Not you, bro. You gotta go back to camp."

Noel slumped. "Why are we doing this?"

"Hell, if I know. I'd rather have a beer and an egg and be sitting in a pub and I don't even drink. Here, can I help you back behind the lines? It's quiet a minute, nah, there go the flash bangs again. Can you roll?"

"I don't think so. Shh."

They heard someone coming through the brush. They were not speaking English. They were speaking quietly in the bush, trying to sneak in back of the Marines ascending the hill. They heard a gasp and realized they were killing the wounded as they came. Noel quietly pulled his knife. Skinwalker laid down his gun, and took out a slingshot. He loaded something into it, put a finger to his lips and slipped away as Noel pulled himself behind a tree and waited. There was a sudden shriek, and it got still. Skinwalker returned.

"Think it's safe enough to leave now," he said quietly.

"What was that?"

"Little thing I learned from an aborigine. These darts have a poison that kills fast but it's not so comfortable-feels like a heavy duty wasp for about 30 seconds, then the heart stops. There were two of them. Now there's none. I scouted around. Think we can walk back if we're careful like."

"So not standard issue? Rats."

"In New Zealand, we sort of modify our packs more than you yanks do." He helped Noel up. Noel suddenly stiffened and threw his knife.

"What?"

"You missed a little person. Let's get my knife and get out of here."

"I miss the safety of the bush back home. All we gots spiders the size of dinner plates and poisonous worms."

"I miss the mountains."

"I told my mum this was a bad idea."

"She wanted you to come to Nam?"

"Thought it might make a man out of me. All that book learning has made me weak, she says."

"You believed her?"

"No, but the draft board was pretty insistent I leave Oxford. Ok, mate. Back home." Limping, arm around each other, they slipped back out of the jungle. "Wish the folks had never left England sometimes."

"You didn't like New Zealand?"

"Like I said, they got earthworms the length of your leg and bird eating spiders. I don't mind the bush so much, but I miss Oxford."

"You got plans after the war?"

"I signed up for more special forces work but not here. Then back to finish the education between tours. I want to eventually join one of the cousin's labs."

"Pretty sure you got that in the bag. Consider yourself a brother, not a cousin."

"If we make it out, I'll look you up."

"Not hard to find us; we just have to make it to the road. Just the road. Jeeps there, maybe a bird to evac us," muttered Noel as he pushed himself from tree to tree with his friend. When they got to the bottom of the hill and across the few feet of woods, just before the road, there was a shot. Skinwalker grunted and stumbled and fell. Noel fell on him. Gunfire broke out and Noel pulled Skinwalker under some brush.

"Where are you hit?

117

"Calf, I think. Hurts like bloody hell." Noel yanked off his undershirt and tied a tourniquet around Skinwalker's leg.

"Any place else?"

"It's enough to stop us. Aren't we a pair, your shoulder, my leg, how in the devil are we going to make the last hundred yards with that sniper out there?"

"Give me your slingshot."

"Back pocket."

Noel pulled it out, studied it. "It'll work. Stay put."

"Like I'm going dancing?"

Noel steadied himself. He took a couple deep breaths. He settled the dart in its place. He lay still and listened.

The sniper waited as well, and then started moving, trying to see his quarry through the trees.

Noel watched and lay low as the sniper got closer, crouching, bouncing from tree to tree, weapon ready, looking for the wounded men. He stood up a little straighter to see better and Noel fired the dart. It hit the sniper in the neck. The sniper grabbed it, gurgled and fell. Noel stumbled back to his friend.

"Good tool that. Might have to get one for meself," he muttered. "Now you lean here on my good side, keep your bad leg between us, and let's get out of here."

"Need no second invite on that," said his cousin. "Hey, guess what? We got a war story for the next Bear feast."

"That we do. Keep sharp." The two men stumbled together, across the field to the road. They fell into the road and lie still along the edge, trying to look dead, feeling nearly there. A Red Cross van, hauling men out if the battle area, stopped and tossed them aboard and charged down the road, away from the battle, towards a waiting helicopter.

Chapter 21

"But I don't understand," began Nurse Violet. She preferred to go by her first name instead of last, and no one seemed to mind in higher command. "That isn't my work. I don't knot bandages like that and I surely don't just throw antiseptic all over a wound. Who on earth got to this dressing?"

"It was that pretty little red haired thang," replied the soldier, looking at the head nurse. "This one didn't do the dressing on this, ma'am."

"Well, you're on her duty roster, not Nurse Obsidian."

"I didn't mind her, ma'am. She's gentle. Asked a lot of questions about the place back home and my folks, real friendly like. She wanted to know if I was related to captain White, since my last names' White, but I ain't. Not related to anyone important that I know of, just my own folks and pa, he's a farmer and Ma keeps house. Sure wish I could have me some of her peach pie right now."

"Violet Grace, clean up this mess. If Corporal Obsidian shows up, send her to my tent."

"Yes, ma'am. And ma'am, May I check the others quickly on my duty roster and see if any of the others have been tampered with? I'd like to know before I get to them." she turned back to the soldier. "Now Soldier White, can you sit up a little? Shoulder wounds just hurt a mite. I've got to fix this so you heal better." Violet took off the mismanaged dressing and threw it away, then carefully cleaned the wound that was starting to fester. The private grunted a couple times and turned white, but he held out. She got it thoroughly cleaned, packed and bandaged, then checked the bedding.

"Your beds still clean but let me just tighten this sheet a bit. There," she said smoothing the pillow. "Now I have some other men to work on, but can I get anything for you?"

"If I could just have paper, I could write home and let them know I'm ok."

"I can do that. You just lie back here and let me check this chart. OK, you're next painkiller isn't due for an hour yet. Let me get the paper." She walked up to the front desk, got a clipboard and several sheets of paper, a couple envelopes and a pen and took it back to the private. Then she went along with her own duties. As she was completing the last man, her Director of Nurses/Commanding Officer was back.

"Violet, have you seen Obsidian?"

"No ma'am. Just working with my boys."

The DON nodded. "Good job. No one else has seen her either. Where do you go next?"

"In fifteen minutes, I'm off duty and thought I'd go catch a shower and eat supper. There's a book screaming my name back at the tent."

"Rest fast. We got wounded arriving in a couple hours. So go get your shower and eat, get off your feet and get dressed again. You'll be needed in surgery."

"I thought Obsidian had surgery detail this week?"

"Not if we can't locate her. If she's gone off to town without notifying me again, I'll bust her down to private, whether the lead surgeon likes it or not.."

The DON stalked her way back to the main medical tent.

Violet turned around. "You boys take care of yourselves. My relief will be here in a few minutes. I actually get to go eat supper."

Violet got her gear from her tent and headed over to the showers. She went in to her assigned stall and found Obsidian already there.

"Hey, don't use up all the hot water," she said cheerfully. "You seen the CO yet? She's been looking for you."

"What would you care? You're a snitch."

"I beg your pardon?"

"Thanks to you, I get to pull an extra shift." Obsidian turned off the water and pulled her towel around her.

"I still have no idea what you're talking about." Another nurse answered. "The DOM called her on the carpet for picking and choosing guys to work with. Obsidian's sure you told on her."

"I did not. The DON came and was checking the men, one of the bandages was on wrong. She asked me what I was thinking when I changed it and I pointed out I hadn't changed it yet; I was three men down and hadn't done this one. The young man told the DON it was a red haired nurse and he didn't say anything bad, just that you'd changed the bandage. Now can I please have the shower? I have to pull a second shift too, in surgery. We got wounded coming in."

"Why are you doing surgery?" demanded Obsidian, not moving from her place. "I'm assigned to surgical."

"I'm assigned because the DON assigned me there; she changed the duty roster. I don't know where you're assigned, and I don't care. Now get out of the way."

Still glaring, Obsidian pushed her way out and bumped hard into Violet, who was ready for the affront. She didn't flinch, just shoved back as Obsidian flounced past.

"Is she really going out dressed only in a towel?" asked one of the other nurses.

"Knowing her, she'll drop the towel on the way back to the tent for some sun," replied another.

Violet got in to the shower and groaned. "Guess it's a cold shower for me."

"You know she's taken three showers this afternoon?" said another nurse. "She runs them out of hot water and moves to another one."

"Really?"

"Anyone reporting it?" asked a third nurse.

"No, but we ought to. This is stupid. She's a pain in the backside. She goes over the charts in the surgery and looks for boys who have money or connections back home and tries to find out where they're going to be and pays special visits to them; she was late to shift the other day and I went to her tent and she was nowhere to be found. She ended up coming out of one of the officers' tents."

"What about her patients?"

"I called an orderly and we took care of the boys, their meds were late, bandages not dressed. I found her afterwards in another tent, chatting up a kid she thought might be related to the CO." The nurse talking turned off her water and started to towel off. "I asked one of the surgeons and he told me they'd had her like here before, looking to make a husband out of someone with some pull. Heard she's done a few tricks as well for officers to get info."

"You think she's a spy?"

"Nah, I heard her once say she was part of a quality control thing. I have no idea what she's talking about." She finished dressing. "Anyone headed for supper?"

A couple nurses joined her and Violet turned on the cold water to rinse her hair. She spoke to another nurse who was just getting into the shower.

"Well, It's hot enough and muggy enough I guess a cold shower isn't a bad thing," sighed Violet. "It might wake me up for the second shift. Anyone know what they're having for supper?"

"I just hope they have coffee this time," remarked another voice. "Gotta go, ladies." The DON stood up from

122

where she was sitting in the back. "You can learn a lot just sitting in the rear of the shower room and I will stop this nonsense, ladies. I have no use for hard working nurses being taken advantage of this way. Not on my watch. Little Miss social climber is about to find the joy in keeping a clean latrine." She left. The other nurses looked at Violet and each other. "I do not think I'd like to be in Obsidian's shoes."

Shaking their heads, they all continued with what they were doing. Violet went back to her tent, finished getting into a clean uniform, and looked longingly at her book. Squaring up her spine, she headed out to eat supper.

Chapter 22

"You any relation to Michael Everett Oberllyn?" asked the pretty red haired nurse as she changed Noel's bandage. He opened his eyes.

"He's my father. He finished his twenty years and is back home."

"Twenty years in special forces? How did he ever survive?" asked the nurse as she checked the wound, added medication and began the re-wrap.

"Bout the same as how everyone survives. He kept his head down."

"You ought to have done that."

"Head was down, shoulder was not."

"Is it true you hauled another guy of the woods with you?"

"I don't leave my brothers behind."

"Spoken like a real Marine." she smiled and got a little closer than Noel thought was strictly needed for the wrapping being done. "It's going to hurt. I don't suppose you worry about pain, being one of those Oberllyn's. You get your orders yet?"

Noel frowned.

"Not that I know of. CO is supposed to come talk to me this afternoon. Say, is that black haired nurse, let's see, flower as I recall, what was her name, anyhow, saw her yesterday. Has a quaint little accent, flutters like a Mother hen."

"Violet? Oh, she's on duty in another tent. She's always late for work."

"Like fun I am!" exclaimed an indignant feminine voice "My shift starts in half an hour. I'm early and Obsidian, I do not need you doing my job!"

"Just trying to be useful."

"Useful only with the cute guys," she scoffed. "Now get off with you to your own patients."

"See you, dreamy," said the red haired nurse as she stood up slowly, giving Noel a wink. "Duty calls."

She left the tent. Violet came over and checked the bandage. "Well, it looks like she did OK by you. How are you feeling? Did she take your temperature, Sargent?"

"No, just changed the bandage. No need to get all worried about it, I suspect there's enough to go around."

Violet shook her head. "She tries to pick and choose her patients, picking the ones with pull or looks and ignoring the rest. I've got no use for ladder climbers. We're supposed to take the clients assigned and it's not the first time she's pulled this. Now, I have this tent of men this afternoon, here, hold this in your mouth. Are you feeling OK? Pain? Headache? Soreness?"

He grunted and talked around the thermometer. "How am I supposed to talk with this in my mouth?"

"Just nod or shake your head. Keep your mouth closed. Here, let's see that. Hmmm, just a low grade temp. Let me get your blood pressure." She efficiently took his vital signs. Then she pulled back the bandage a bit. "No sign of infection."

"Except around my heart muscle."

"Excuse me? You have a cardiac condition? It's not on the chart."

"I have a flower growing out of my chest."

"Excuse me? Are you hallucinating?"

He sighed. "I take it my pick-up lines don't work with nurses?"

"Pick up..., oh, you silly man. No, you're a patient. I can't date you, love you or anything. Got to stay totally professional."

"You said love, I heard you."

"You are hearing every third word."

"Just so long as there's hope, I can do this."

"Now listen, Sargent Oberllyn," she began just as an orderly barked out, "Officer present in the ward!"

She stood up quickly, nearly dropping her thermometer.

"At ease, people." said the commanding officer. "As you were. Oberllyn, how are you feeling?"

"Fair to middling, sir."

"I'd hate to report back to your Da that I'd let his boy get hurt."

"He's retired, sir."

"No one retires in the Oberllyn family. They just go underground."

"If you wish, sir. Sorry I can't get up."

"Are you finished with this man, nurse?"

"Oh, yes, sir. I have other patients. With your permission, sir." Violet scurried off a few beds down and started to work on a dressing. The Commanding officer looked up. "No way to have privacy in here. Son, you object to coming over to my command tent? You hurt too much? I can have someone carry you."

"Are we doing a debriefing while I'm under the influence?"

"You on pain meds?"

Noel's eyes wandered as he nodded. "That and nurses, sir."

"Got some lookers right now. I need to know what you found out there. No one else in your group seems to know what they saw."

"They had flash bangs, lots of bullets, typical Cong traps going on. It was confusing."

"And?"

"I think from what I saw they're heading up for a large offensive shortly." he said quietly. The CO sat down on the edge of the cot and leaned closer. "I overheard some of the men talking about an offensive for Saigon."

"We're withdrawing our people as fast as we can but there's not enough planes or choppers or anything. You know the morale is low, and drug use is impossible-we're losing men to just carelessness. You and the others here are going to be transported tomorrow nearer the airport, the entire camp is bugging out. We've signed the Peace accord in Paris; we want all wounded out of here by end of this week. It's been one helluva mess over here. I was in Korea, I was in other skirmishes and I never saw anything like this snafued up, batch of incompetence."

"Commander White, it's been an honor to serve under you."

"You just get home safe, son. And tell you what; I'll see you're shipped out in the same chopper as that pretty little nurse over there. You're both going home to the same camp to recover. No need to be shy."

"I don't plan to be, sir."

"Rest well, son. I know her family; she's good stock. You could do worse. Say hi to your Daddy for me when you get home."

"I will. And thank you sir." Noel paused. "Sir, where's Cpl. David Skinwalker?"

"Who?"

"The man who came in with me; got shot in the leg?"

"He's already been shipped out to Germany to recover. Aussie's took him over."

"He's going to recover?"

128

"Sure will, son. His leg's going to need some hefty surgery and physical therapy, but he'll be back among the kangaroos in no time."

"I think he said he'd re-enlisted."

"Yes, but can't tell you more than that. He's still special forces, like you. When you get stateside, you might ask the chaplain to try and locate him for you. They have more pull in some of that stuff than I do. Right now, with all the evacuation, it's a gawd awful mess out there."

"I'll just call home. Mom can find him."

The General laughed. "If anyone could do it, it'd be your Mother. Woman can ferret out a flea from a long haired cat. You take it easy, son."

"Did we take the hill sir?"

"Taken and blown to bits. Lot of cong meeting their maker this last few days. Now you just relax,. Your evac's at 6 tomorrow. Nurse?"

"Sir?"

"Weren't you on duty last night when these men were brought in?"

"Yes sir, I was in surgery."

"How many shifts they making you work?"

"It's ok sir, I got a nap. I get off in two hours and I can rest then."

"Lot of wounded lately."

"Yes, sir. It's a bloody war."

"Yes, it is. Aide?" The CO's aide came forward. "Look, I'm writing these orders, I want them typed and ready for signature in fifteen minutes, This soldier and this nurse are leaving the next transport out. That's at 6 am."

"Sir? I'm not due to be sent home for six months." replied Violet.

"Not home. Reassigned. I want you to take care of this man and a couple others I'm listing specifically. You have just become a military private duty nurse. Both of you are heading for Germany."

Chapter 23

The injured, nurses and orderlies were loaded into the cargo plane which took off for Germany before dawn the next day. All the soldiers were being reassigned; some mustered out, some to heal up and go to other places. Violet went from stretcher to stretcher being sure her men were safely settled in.

"Hello, Violet," smiled Noel. "Glad to see you could make it."

"I was ordered here, just like you, so don't get funny with me. Now are you properly strapped, let's see, yes, yes and yes. " She turned around, checked the next man and went down the line. Noel watched her, smiling to himself.

"She's quite the looker, ain't?" asked a low voice next to him.

"That she is. You done with the military?"

"Naw, just heading back for a breather and then out I go again. Yourself?"

"I suspect I've got more work to do before I rest. Names' Noel."

"I'm Malcom. I was supposed to ship with the other kiwis but missed the flight. Lost my main man, tall skinny fella named Skinwalker-you know him?"

"He's my cousin, more like brother. Makes you a friend."

"You don't say? You the bloke got him out of the mess back there?"

"We sort of hobbled out together."

"I appreciate it. His Da would kill me if that youngster got mangled. Heard he shipped yesterday?"

"I heard the same. He's a good man to have in a fight."

"We're right proud of the young'un'. You ever down under?"

"Not yet, but would like to."

"Look the family up when you do. I'm Malcom Wolfe. Specialist first class, tend to blow things up."

"You can look up ours as well. We're spread out a bit over the world. My grandmom and Da are in Washington, got cousins in Colorado, California, North Carolina, England, Down under..."

Marvin got an odd look on his face. "You're one of those Oberllyns, ain't?

"Yes, I am."

"I met an uncle of yourn. Name of Wildfox, and then met the fella Skinwalker-you Americans do go for odd names."

"Seems like everyone I meet from Aussieland is a Malcom. And Malcolm, I think Skinwalker was your contact with us, but you can use me as well. Let me know of whatever it was your supposed to be doing for us. Right now, I know you're on Da's list of contacts for possible reconnaissance but right now, we both have to get well."

"Agreed. That sure is a looker, and the redhead? My blood pressure has a problem I think and I do believe I'd best have it checked."

Noel laughed. "I prefer the quiet brunette. She's got less miles on her, if you get my drift."

"I'm not figuring on settling down so the red will do fine to tease a bit. Just the thing to lift me spirits."

Just as Violet finished with her men, she looked up at a clicking sound. Obsidian was sitting in the hold, strapping herself in, smiling at her.

"I see you lucked out too," she smiled. "I'm heading out of that hell hole back there and being sent to Germany. I'll finish out my enlistment at a nice quiet Vet hospital. I've got a job waiting when I come out. What about you?"

"I have six more months and hadn't quite decided to re-enlist. I don't know. I thought to get some more education, possibly a masters in social work. The Army would pay for that if I stayed. I'd like to try and help folks. By the way, are your men secured?" Obsidian stretched and evaded the question.

"That's crazy talk. With your skills, you could do something with your life." She remarked.

"I am doing something with my life. Last I looked, I was saving lives. And your patients?"

"Most of them inconsequential." The engines started up. She leaned closer.

"Since you're done with yours and I'm already strapped down, you could do them for me, Violet. Listen, I could get you an interview with the folks hiring me. They can use good operatives."

"I'm a nurse. Not an operative. Thanks for the invite. But you need to go and get your men strapped down."

"How 'bout if I take the guys on this side and you over there?"

"We've got our assigned clients. Besides, I did my side already. Get your butt in gear."

"There's no DON here to keep us from changing. I'd rather work over here and I am." She took a file form somewhere and started filing her nails.

" This side is done and you know it. Why do work over?"

"Well, for one thing, you got that hunk Oberllyn down there, totally conscious and right next to him is Malcolm Wolfe: his parents own Wolfe Industries back home. He's the one got me the interview with his mom."

"Well, I intend to follow orders. If you want to talk to them OK, but I intend to take care of my patients. So after you've done yours, you want to come visit someone, it's a free country but really, I won't take responsibility for your clients and you ought not expect it of mine."

"Well, you're just a fussy prig, that's all." Seeing a Captain come in with a duty roster clipboard, Obsidian jumped up, concern written on her face and dashed over to her men and superficially checked the men's stretchers. While being watched, she tightened some straps, attached others. Violet shook her head and then moved closer to the front of the plane and strapped down near to Malcom and Noel. She felt the plane rolling, turning, accelerating and climbing as she was pushed back into her seat. Her blood pressure seemed to rise with it, recalling all the stories of how the most dangerous time was lift off, when the most planes got shot down by the enemy. *If they can get this plane to cruising altitude, we'll be OK,* she thought. *Lord, just get us up to the flight path home. Send us some angel to guide our path. I don't know why you've taken me out of this situation and why I'm going somewhere else, but where ever I go, just help me to serve others and You.* She gave a little cheep as the plane hit an air pocket and dropped, then recovered and thundered higher. From the back of the plane, Obsidian cursed as she sat down hard and strapped in. All the men seemed intact and the orderlies as well. The Captain had strapped in before and was writing notes on his clipboard sheets.

"You OK, darling?" said Noel. "It's always a mite bumpy."

"Just praying we don't get shot down."

"You pray much?"

"Every day. And yourself?"

He smiled. "It keeps me together when nothing else could. I'm from Virginia mostly, by way of California, Indiana, and a lot of other places.."

"I was born in Maine. I was raised in different places, but my tribe is centered in middle Ohio."

"Tribe?"

"I'm a Lenape."

134

"Really?"

"Yes, really. Does it bother you?"

"My great Grandmother was a Lenape."

"Is that a line?"

"Yoh niis jos! Wele Kishku."(Hello, it is a good day)

"Ktalënixsi hàch "(Do you speak lenape?) she asked in surprise. "My mom is the Nation's Mother."

"Mahtiti shëkw" (A little) "My Grandpa taught me, and his Grandpa taught him. I use trade sign better."

She smiled at him. "That's grand. I don't speak as much as I'd like but my mom was a native speaker. Who was your great Grandmother?"

"Her name was Genevieve. It's a long family story." he answered. "She came to the United States by way of Scotland. And yours?"

"Battle of Fallen Timbers took out my ancestors; one boy was raised with Quakers. I'm his descendant. I reconnected as a child when mom reconnected. It's a long story."

"I'd love to hear it some time. We could exchange stories, maybe when I'm no longer a patient?"

"That would be nice. You don't often meet someone traditional and it's good to treasure the meetings."

"Do you know grandfather Storyteller?"

"He was at my sister's naming ceremony. A grand old elder."

"He's dear to us."

Just then, someone groaned and Violet unfastened her belt. "Someone needs me. I'll be back soon."

"Looking forward to it."

He watched as she left to go help a soldier who was sweating with pain.

"She's a looker all right, maybe even a keeper. You getting serious?" asked his friend Malcolm.

"Believe I am. She hits all the checkmarks, religion, ancestry, skill, stubborn and she's not hard on the eyes. Also seems level headed."

Malcolm nodded. "Yep, I'd say she was a keeper. What do you think of Red?"

"Obsidian? Sort of the kind that walks over folks to get ahead. Got no need for someone like that."

"She's got eyes on you."

"Yeah, I've seen it, don't like it."

"You don't mind me having some fun with her?"

"She's not a keeper."

"Sounds good. That fish has just been thrown into my pond. Let's see how she swims…"

"Just stay away from my lady."

"Yours already?"

"If I have anything to say about it."

The captain took the seat between the two men.

"Gentlemen, I'm Dr. Steven Zion. I'll be escorting you to the hospital and Mr. Oberllyn, I need to speak to you in private at some point. I have a message from your family."

Noel raised his eyebrows. "Really? You have a letter for me?"

"Not so much a letter. More of a telegram."

"Wow, Da must really be going primitive if he's using a telegraph."

"Well, it looks something like a telegram. Has a lot of stops in it."

"Well, since I don't do code," Malcolm said. "Might as well give it to him. I can't read it."

"I do code," said Obsidian. "I'll bet I can help." The plane hit some light turbulence and she fell down in front of the captain.

Noel cleared his throat. "I believe this was a private conversation. Didn't invite you."

136

"Oh, come on, now," she wheedled. "I'm good at this, I really am. Among other things."

"So why are you a nurse?"

The plane shifted and bumped in the turbulence. Obsidian fell against the captain. He stood her up. "Nice try, nurse. I don't have the message on me, and I don't appreciate being frisked but hey, you want to play sometime, look me up." He looked down at Noel. "Your Da said, 'Red Prayer ties on the old tree.' I don't have the faintest idea."

"I'd like to see the note he sent."

"And I will give it to you at the hospital. Right now, we're going to go look after our passengers." He strong armed Obsidian away towards the back of the men and started directing her to different men to help.

Violet returned.

"That looked different," she said quietly. "What on earth is she getting into now?"

"Irritating officers," replied Malcolm. "I was hoping she'd try to irritate me."

"She already has you," scoffed Violet. "You got her an interview with your folks' business. So she has what she wants and she needn't bother with you anymore. My guess is either Davis back there, who's Da is a big wig in a company or Michealis over there, whose Da is a general."

"What about me?" asked Noel.

"You're spoken for but don't think she isn't going to try."

"I'm spoken for?"

"Yes, you're my particular trial to deal with, and she doesn't need to mess that up. Now, both of you try to get some rest if you can with this blasted bucking plane."

"Hey, any day you don't get shot down is a good day." replied Noel. "Sing me a lullaby?"

"I can give you a shot to keep you quiet."

"Not the same nuance," he smiled. "But considering my pain level, and the fact I can't do anything, I'll take it. Seriously."

Chapter 24

Once they arrived in Germany, the men were quickly put into ambulances and driven to the Landstuhl regional medical center, taken to their rooms and admitted. Obsidian was put on the schedule to work on surgery floor, another section of the building from the men she wanted to shadow. The orders Violet was given put her directly into the ward where Noel was recuperating. She was assigned he and five other men who were to be given special treatment. The six men were her ward alone on her shift.

The Captain from the plane came to the ward with her.

"Nurse Violet, these men are given special treatment not because of their wounds but because they're special forces and their security clearance is such that they can't be in the common population. You're here, not only as nurse but to help act as a bodyguard. We know you have marital arts training. You will keep a sidearm on at all times."

"A sidearm? In a hospital ward?"

"Absolutely. The door is to be kept locked. There is a rotating list of code words to get the door opened. You won't be here long, and most of your men are ambulatory, I think, so you will be accompanied to the mess. Guards will come to take you."

"That is really odd," Violet spurted the words out. "I mean, with all due respect sir, I'm a nurse."

"I know. That's why no one will suspect you of being anything else. Go ahead, pass meds, change dressings, get them well and able to move but be on your toes. You will work 8 hours a day; you will be relieved by two other similarly trained nurses."

"Do I know them?"

"I rather doubt it. You will live here on campus in the nurses' quarters. Your bags have been taken over already, here's your door key. For now, go see to the men. Your shift is over in a little over two hours and I'll have your replacement come and someone with him to escort you to your quarters."

"Thank you sir, I think."

She put the key in her pocket, took the duty key for the door and went in.

Noel and Malcolm looked up, as did David Skinwalker and a man she'd not met.

"Skinwalker wasn't sent to Kiwi land! Isn't that grand?" called Noel.

"I'm glad, I think. Um, and soldier, I don't know you?"

"Sam Black. I'm special forces. They tried to blow me up. I objected with prejudice and took a bullet." Her other two men were unconscious with head wounds. "Those are my buddies. They weren't as lucky as me. I got them out though." said Sam. "They're going to get better, right?"

"That's up to God and the doctors and themselves," said Violet firmly. She checked their IV's and marked on the charts.

"Now this is a locked ward so the only folks coming in will be nurses and doctors."

"Why are we locked?" asked Sam.

"I'm not really sure, I was just told."

Noel touched her hand and said softly, "Violet, you packing?"

She answered softly, "I'm afraid so and not quite sure why but there are two armed guards outside this ward. Maybe you can tell me?" Noel shook his head. "Did the Captain give you anything for me?" he asked Violet.

"No."

"That's not good."

"Hey, mate," said Malcolm.

"Yes?"

"That red haired nurse wouldn't stop watching the Captain so on one of his trips by he slipped this into my pocket for you." He extended his hand over. "It's still folded up." Violet leaned over and took it, then handed it to Noel.

He opened it and studied what was written. As he studied, Violet made her rounds, checking bandages, marking charts. She chatted with the other men. She finally got back to Noel. He lay back with his eyes closed.

"Taking a rest is a good idea." she started.

"I'm not. I'm writing on the walls of my college classroom. It's how I decipher things. I close my eyes and put it all up there for sorting on moving blackboards."

"I see. Does it work?"

"Most times."

"Is your note in code? Can I get you some paper?"

"Yes and no. Let me think."

"Sounds good. Supper is in half an hour though, so think fast." She left his side and checked the men in comas again.

She looked at her written instructions, made a note of the day's password. *It says here I am to memorize the password and instructions,. Tear them up and burn them over there in that can. This just gets odder and odder."* she thought to herself. *"OK, so today's password is island. Be nice if they'd left me matches...wait, here's some in the can. OK, lets see, good night, all the men in this room are in intelligence. I'm in a room full of spies, our spies but gee whiz, 007 times six? Really? So guess I better burn this. Wait, let me read that again. Noel is a member of the Oberllyn think tank on loan to the US government. That means he's going to away soon. Ah well, a girl could have hoped for a normal guy..."* Violet read it all over again and took it over and burned it as ordered.

"What was that?" asked Malcolm. "You not have some cigarettes on you? Or was it that sage stuff Noel carries round?"

"Don't smoke, sorry. Just some things I had to make disappear." Malcolm got an odd look on his face. "OK, doll, whatever you say. You wouldn't happen to know where that pretty red haired nurse went?"

"'Fraid not."

"OK. Maybe I'll see her in the mess hall."

"Maybe. Can you walk to the mess hall?"

"I thought maybe they had a wheelchair?"

"Anything's possible." she went back to notating.

There was a knock at the door. She went to it. She pushed the button on the intercom.

"Island." came a voice. Violet opened the door.

"My name is Theodore Wildfox." he said quietly. "The Captain and I are here to see Noel." Wildfox was pushing a wheelchair. "Come along, Noel."

"Captain?"

"It's fine, nurse." assured the Captain. "His security clearance checks out and he, I and Noel need to debrief. We'l be in the meeting room two doors down."

"I can walk," said Noel, struggling up.

"No, you can't. Hospital rules," replied the Captain.

"Can I at least have something that covers my backside? It's drafty in here." The nurse went to the closet and got him a striped cotton robe.

"So now I look like a prisoner on leave." he joked. "I'l be seeing you soon, guys. Hello, Uncle WildFox."

"Afternoon, Noel. Let's get this accomplished. Malcolm you're next."

"Nice to know I get a turn." he grinned. "Don't let the buzzards wear you down, brother."

"No worries," replied Noel. Violet shut the door and locked it behind them.

Chapter 25

Angelica frowned as she looked at the report that had just arrived in her lab.

"Noel's coming home," she thought to herself. "I suspect his family knows already but I'll just give them a call. This other data though, this troubles me and I think I'd best call Uncle Glen in."

"Melissa, I'm making a short jaunt out to the farm." she told her receptionist. "You can take the rest of the day if you want. I won't be back til morning.

"Thank you ma'am. I want to get these entries put up first and I'll head for home."

Out on the interstate, Angelica frowned. Taking an exit, she headed towards Washington and Glen's office.

As she walked in, Adam was just saying goodbye to Glen.

"Just the two men I need to see," she smiled. "What do you think of this intel I just got?" She handed a folder over to Glen Oberllyn, the newly minted head of Washington operations. Adam had been giving him the last report on his way home where, he fervently hoped, his own retirement could begin.

Glen frowned. "Are your informants accurate?"

"President Nixon is making an appearance at a fundraiser at the Hilton Hotel in two days. The secret Service have been going over it with a fine tooth comb to be sure there's no way that his speech can do anything but just raise money. They've

got people already stationed around there. However, this inte
included maps and grids of the area, definite planning."

"You think they're trying to take him out?"

"We know that Ford's a good man but he isn't going t
be able to handle China."

Adam considered. "There are those who think we ough
not open up talks with China. It's less than six months til hi
trip."

"The fundraiser is sold out." replied Adam. "We've bee
asked to have a presence."

"I think we may need to be more than a presence.
replied Angelica. "Is our brother going to be home from
Germany?"

"He was injured. He needs to have time off, regroup hi
personal force." Glen stated with what he hoped was finality
He knew his wife really wanted Noel home for a time, more t
reassure herself that her son was fine.

"He is supposed to be released to rejoin us. The questio
is whether it will be soon enough to help with this." Angelic
pressed on.

"I understand that he and his intended were able t
accomplish a job for us on the Rhine while recovering?" aske
Adam.

"His intended?"

"Appears he has found someone to be serious about. Hi
mom can't wait to meet her."

"I can't either," replied Angelica. "The question now i
can he be home in a day?"

Just then, the phone rang by Glen's hand. He picked i
up. "Yes? Really? That is most welcome news, dear. Tell him
will be there in a short time and to relax. He did? Is she pretty
Grand. Can you have her fitted with a green ball gown by thi
afternoon? Ouch! You don't have to get quite that enthusiasti
on the phone, dear. We're attending a fundraiser. I'll explai

when I get home. Please see that my and Noel's tuxes are ready for wearing. He did? That's simply outstanding. See you shortly. OK, not too shortly."

"Noel and his intended just arrived by surprise and the wife is ecstatic. Rustle us up tickets for tonight's event, Angelica. Noel, Violet, Angelica, wife, myself, maybe just get the family a table near the front. Let's get a plan together and we can just call it a business expense."

"How much do we know about his intended?" frowned Adam.

"I sent Noel a message two months ago while he was recuperating. He took a short leave with the young lady and was able to get on board a boat doing the tourist thing down the Rhine river. On the boat were two hidden Nazi operatives, heading out to fly to South America. They were apprehended, not by Noel, but by his girlfriend who appears to have a photographic memory of sorts and really hates Nazis. She'd seen their photos a few years ago as some of the most wanted. Franz Strangl was listed. He and one of Speer's men were in hiding but had come back to see their old home before exiling to South America. Noel and Violet made positive ID and captured them, turning them over to the police in Cologne."

"Excellent. I take it she acquitted herself well?"

"Very well. She took two of the body guards down herself. Of course, she threw some red haired lady into the Rhine river right after. The gendarmes there take a dim view of that. She got into a little trouble with her CO over it, but we smoothed it out. Noel covered for her. It turns out that Violet has a black belt. She also has a couple national titles for small bore rifles and indoor pistols." replied Glen as he looked at the maps of the hotel area.

"Sounds promising." said Angelica.

"And she's knockout pretty." said Glen. "She has a Master's in surgical nursing and is headed back to get another

145

master's, possibly a doctorate, in Social work." he answered. "So intelligent as well. Somewhat opinionated, tribal member, Christian, just a little hotheaded and possessive of what's hers. The red haired one she tossed was making a play for Noel's attention..."

"Wait, What? Tribal as well?" asked Angelica.

"Yes, and Christian."

"Good night, where did he find this paragon?" asked Glen.

"In a just behind the lines nursing facility."

"Experience doesn't hurt either." answered Adam. "Are you going to need me on this little escapade?"

"I surely hope not, unless you need one last fling?"

"Lillian would kill me. We're heading for Colorado tomorrow. Our stuff has already been shipped."

"Then I'll see you in ten years at the reunion. You take care, Da."

"And you keep me posted when you can. Don't make yourselves strangers." The men hugged briefly, Angelica hugged Adam next. He left, leaving the home office in the capable hands of his son Glen and the next generation.

"Angelica, we'll need you not dressed up as an ingénue this time, but possibly in the background."

"I can do that."

"Let's look at the itinerary for the President for that day."

Chapter 26

Adam pulled into the house he and his wife had built years before near the lab in Colorado.

"I am so looking forward to just relaxing for the next twenty or so years." he remarked as he got out and stretched. He went over and opened his wife's door. "How about you, Lillian?"

"I'm going to finally get my quilt tops done," she declared. "I can't wait to get into my craft room. I cut them all out on our last vacation and they are just neatly stacked, waiting and now I don't have to wait anymore. Even if we get snowed in, I've got enough project cut out for the next year or two or three."

"I've always had a hankering to raise some chickens. GrandDa always had them. I think my next project will be to suss out a place to put a chicken house. Some Rhode Island reds, maybe a few Orphingtons, a couple Wyandottes, Aracauanas for color,"

"It has to be accessible if there's a blizzard."

"South side of the house then," he said cheerfully. "Lots of pines there to block the snow. Ah, wife, just look at it. Isn't it the prettiest place you've ever seen?"

"It's been a long time coming. Help me get the bags?"

"Surely." Adam went to the back of the car and pulled out the suitcases just as the front door opened.

"Welcome home," cried their maid Julie. "We've got it all unpacked. Supper will be on in two minutes and just let's get those traveling bags up to your room."

"Sounds marvelous! Smells divine!" exclaimed the Oberllyns as they entered their new home.

Adam and his wife went up the two steps to the porch and entered their home. They'd been working on it, on and off, for twenty years, spending summers and vacations here, continuing the plan. They'd finished installing an indoor pool and hot tub complex out back just last summer, and during the last couple years while they slowly divested all their duties to their children, they'd been doing the landscaping and putting in raised beds to make it easy as they grew older to still garden. There were walking paths set up and a bomb proof, bullet proof safe room in the cellar, right next to the armory and survival supplies; just what one needs when retiring from a career of espionage. The retirement house was five miles from one of the family labs, so Adam could still go over and poke around, get into Angelica Summermoon's way and keep his mind busy. The family gym was now at their house so they'd have company nearly every day as the differing members came to the dojo to work out and into the pool to cool off. With any luck, they'd reach a great old age like their ancestors.

After a great dinner, they thanked their helpers and helped with clean-up and they were finally alone.

"You want to go skinny-dipping in our pool?" suggested Adam with a mischievous look on his face as he put his arms around his wife Lillian.

"Remember we have to wait a half hour after we eat to get in the water so we don't get cramps. By my reckoning, we have fifteen more minutes, since you insisted on eating more while we cleaned up."

"I can do fifteen minutes. I'm locking the doors and setting on the alarm, and calling the dogs in, and getting naked and relaxing with my wife and no interruptions…" And then the doorbell rang.

Chapter 27

Glen stood at the door of the hotel in the predark twilight. He was flanked by two tribal members and a Secret Serviceman, who were watching for the convoy of Presidential vehicles to come. On the rooftops of the other hotels and businesses around them, the police swat teams from the local departments stood next to Secret Servicemen. Inside, the Secret Service were already stationed. Glen spoke into his wrist communicator.

"Is everyone in place?"

"Affirmative," replied each of his operatives.

"Anything odd about any of the other details?"

"Glen, I'm in place behind the dais curtain, behind where the President will be. I can see the hall from where I am standing and nothing appears out of place. There is however a person who appears to be one of the waiters that has placed what may be bugs on some of the tables?" The Secret Service person with Glen remarked, "That's one of ours and yes, those are scattered listening devices at the President's request."

"I see. And the Swat members are in place down here. Has everyone been screened?"

"About as well as we can do with the guest list. There's a chance that one of them may inadvertently bring a date or an aide that's not kosher, but we take care of one problem at a time."

"Glen, this is Green bird one," said a quiet voice. "Is this working?"

"Sure enough, Violet."

"Never had one of these toys. And doesn't Noel look fine in a tux?"

"He cleans up well," answered Glen.

"And why is she using official communications for chatter?" asked the Secret Service man, who was carrying a hand radio phone and more than a little envious of the watch communicators.

"Just letting you boys know up front Noel just finished stashing a couple goons in the closet to the left of the podium for pick up later. They were dressed as waiters. They had C-4 in their pockets, with igniters laced in. We took that. Noel has it in a bucket of ice now, and it's sitting behind a planter. And he's on his way back and looks just fine. The two fellows may have been only a backup. Just as he went down, one of them mentioned the others had gotten thorough. He said something about hitting below the belt?"

"What others?" demanded the Secret Service commander.

"Don't know. I hit him pretty hard with that vase. Good thing it wasn't Ming or anything, probably K-Mart blue light special. Broke gloriously over his head. We're going to mingle a bit and see what else we can find."

Glen raised his eyebrow at his tribal men and motioned with his chin. They sprinted off.

"I'm having them take the prisoners to a less public closet," he said quietly. "You have men stationed on the back loading dock?"

"Absolutely."

"Tell them to expect the first of possibly several packages to deal with."

"Will do." he looked again at the watch. "Where'd you get that?"

"Adam made them for us before he retired. Useful things, free up the hands for work. Pretty sturdy: not good under water though. We're working on a waterproof case."

"How many times you talk underwater?"

Glen considered. "You have a point there. Here comes the motorcade." Both men looked at the street, noted the officers and agents meeting the motorcade, surrounding President Nixon as he waved to the crowd and went inside the hotel. *"So far, nothing happening here,"* thought Glen to himself. *"Hope it's all clear inside but guess it won't be."*

Angelica Summermoon stood still behind the curtain, watching the crowd. Everyone had been seated now; the waiters and waitresses were lined up on the sides, having served out the plates and drinks, and everyone was waiting the entrance of the President. She scanned the crowd, the waiters, the agents in the hall. The din of people talking, eating, was making her jumpy. Noel and his lady and the family were seated at an off center table near the Presidential table. She was a pretty lady. Fair skinned, gorgeous hair, and the teal green, mermaid dress was stunning. Angelica swiveled her eyes back to the surroundings. There was a commotion in the back of the room. She knew it was to draw people's attention away from what actually happened up front as the President, led off by his chief of staff, entered the room on the side and took his place at the head table, just in front of her. Nixon looked uneasy and somewhat stiff as he waved to the crowd. He spoke to his aide.

"I feel like there's eyes on me."

"Sir, there are five hundred people who've paid $5000 each to eat this meal with you. Of course there are eyes."

"No, it seems like something else."

"If there is sir, Secret Service will be in the line of fire. The agents have your back." The President sat down. He reached forward nervously for a drink of water.

There was a sudden cry of "Gun! Nine O'clock!" as Summermoon tore the fake curtains down in front of her and dove for the President, knocking him to the ground and covering his body as three agents tackled a waiter who had been standing at the end of the Presidential table. He had pulled a small North American arms buckle gun out of his belt buckle from under his jacket. No one had thought to look for a small decorative weapon. At the same time, Noel had knocked over a table next to him and was sitting on another man who had had another small revolver. Violet had a lady in a choke hold having divested her of a knife she had tried to use on Noel. The Secret Service hustled the President out of the hall and out from under Summermoon.

In a few minutes, all was calm. The three protesters had joined the two already in custody, there had been a table by table check, and Angelica was asked to stay and eat with her cousin Noel. She sat at the table, keeping her eyes open as a Secret serviceman had taken her place behind the President. Glen joined them.

"Never had much use for this rubber chicken they serve at these things." he remarked.

"Still, the beans aren't bad," answered Noel. "Better than what I've been eating the last few months.

"I think it's lovely," said Violet.

"Thanks for keeping that lady off my back."

"I was not about to have her get blood all over such a nice tux." she replied as she chewed on a roll. "I don't think I've met you?"

"I'm Summermoon," replied Angelica. "But white name is Angelica. Folks call me Angel."

"How did you notice the gun?"

"Something the men you took down with the C-4 said." she replied. "Hitting below the belt. No way could he get close enough to do that but if he was carrying something in his belt or on it..."

"Makes sense. Noel, the man at our table?"

"He was supposed to be a news reporter. He said he had to get his recorder out to record the speech. He reached in his vest to get it, but we'd been briefed there was to be no recordings and none of the other reporters were sitting at a table, they were all back in the lobby. I realized the thing he was pulling out was the wrong shape to be any kind of recorder and tossed the table."

"And the woman must have been in on it because when you went down on the man, she pulled the stiletto out of her purse and lunged for you," replied Violet nodding.

"But she didn't reckon on you keeping my back," he smiled at her. "We do make a good team."

Glen cautioned. "Keep your eyes peeled, but Nixon is only supposed to make a half hour speech and he's starting now. Violet, I need to see you in my office after this?"

"I'm on leave right now from the military."

"I know. You just have Noel fetch you around."

"Glen, did you follow up on the other data?"

"Absolutely. We picked up the cell this afternoon. There are folks on the way to take them out as we speak. They're distracted waiting to hear from their comrades in here, and we'll have them in custody shortly."

"The President doesn't look much the worse for wear," remarked Violet.

"Being knocked to the ground and hidden under a pretty lady hardly qualifies as traumatic, I'd say," he answered, looking at his sister across the table with a grin. "Violet, kick that man!" she retorted.

"Ouch!" Noel gulped." What for?"

"We ladies have to stick together," Violet said demurely, eyes laughing as she smiled at Angelica, who held up her wine glass in recognition.

Chapter 28

Adam went to answer the door. He opened it in a not quite as friendly mood as he should have been, but shortly changed.

"Jerome! I wasn't expecting you! Come in, come in, tell me what you know, won't take long. Lillian, come see our first company!"

Lillian hurried in as Jerome stepped inside.

"I'm not here on good news, I'm afraid. Last night, while driving home from a prayer meeting, Mom and Da's little car got hit by a semi-truck. They driver had had one too many bennies to stay awake and never even saw the car he ran over. The medics say they died instantly. We're all trying to gather as much of the family as possible to go bury them in the family cemetery in California."

Adam looked stunned.

"I don't know what to say," remarked Lillian. "We just saw them at the reunion a couple years ago and they looked great. Sure, Garrette was getting up there, but Genevieve was hale and hearty as those horses she liked riding around. Do the others know?"

"I've got people delivering the news as we speak. Can you two fly out tomorrow? Glen has a couple things to finish at the Washington office but is leaving in the afternoon. Michael's son Noel is on a medical leave of absence and will be heading out. I think only I'm here from the overseas branch of the family; Wildfox is joining me, Helen's already here with me. We'll see who else can come."

157

"I was so looking forward to the next reunion and it won't seem the same without the folks."

"If it hadn't have been for the driver being high, they'd still be with us."

"Do you want to stay the night?"

"I'd appreciate it. I know you just got moved in yourself and I can get room in town,"

"Nonsense. We're family. We got room always. You bring the wife right in here. Have you eaten?"

"Yeah, but I'd not turn down some hot tea right now."

"I can get that in just a minute. Chamomile or mint?"

"Whatever, just put some of Da's honey in it if you have it."

"He shipped that honey to all of us from the farm," sighed Lilian. "Sort of a taste of love from them all out in the home place."

The others nodded as they sat quietly in front of the big picture windows, overlooking the forest and sipped their tea deep in their thoughts.

Chapter 29

The reunion in 1980 was a noisy affair. Noel had married Violet Grace and she had been adopted into his branch of the tribe and he adopted into hers. Noel had left active service and was working for the firm. Violet had gone back to school and gotten her Doctorate in Social Work and was starting a career in government at Health and Human Services while beginning to raise her sons KaiDante and Gabriel and her daughter Jasmine. Glen and his wife had added a child to their family whom they named Lacey Myststorm. Glen, after all the new babies had been added to the family list, stood up and intoned quietly.

"We remember those who have gone before. Our parents Genevieve and Garrette Oberllyn, died in a car accident in 1975. Our brother Adam, died in a plane accident in 1977, leaving us bereft of his wisdom. The wars worldwide took several of the children of our families and we grieve but carry on. Noel has left the military and is taking Adam's place as liaison with the government and head of the laboratories. Jerome's oldest David Skinwalker is to study with the Ute brothers in Utah. He completed his studies in England and it is thought he would do well to be better grounded in our own people's heritage. After a while, he will rejoin the firm and go to Australia to live there and set up our network. Jerome remains in England heading up the work there. We ask the good Lord above watch over this family as we try to keep our country and ourselves free and safe from harm. It's now time for elders meeting. Children and those not family heads, please go out and enjoy the feast prepared by our most capable cooks. They've placed it in the yard under the old Oak tree on the picnic tables.

That oak has been there since this farm was established back in 1856. We will join you shortly." as the children ran out, and their parents followed, leaving just the chief people in the firm Glen said quietly,

"Now Angelica has a report. I warn you, it is troubling."

Summermoon stood. "Before my father died, he had discovered that the underground movement that had been behind some of the recent wars had apparently infiltrated our government. Through judicious use of resources, we have been able to weaken that movement. They call themselves the Brotherhood, though they are always headed by a woman. We have been able to give enough information to certain government entities to alleviate some of their power and they are not particularly happy with us. Evil likes to work in the dark and we have been shining lights on them, taking down their cells and interrupting their communications. I am sending around a list of people we feel are in contact and possibly being influenced by these people. We are also sending intel on the basic structure of the organization. They recently had a change of power within and a new person has stepped into the void caused by some internal dissension. Notice that they are heavily into the occult, and that they try to come across as ecologists and forward thinking people, aligning themselves with the new Age movement. We think their next move is going to be against the economy of the planet, although we are not certain in what form that's going to be. They seem to be attempting to influence the world wide supply of oil and power. They are definitely against Israel."

"These are pretty important people you're accusing here," remarked Glen as he read the pages given.

"They are. They've been able to gain the ears of senators and their lobbyists are some of the best. They work mostly in free countries where they can populate and spread their lies easily in the free press. They do not seem to do as well under dictators, although they themselves are basically a dictatorship. I will give you time to read the papers. Then I need them back. I need to destroy the copies. We cannot allow this out of this room." She went over and stood by a shredder, ready to retrieve back the copies and destroy them.

"We need to put more people on this." said Glen.

Angelica nodded. "We are getting that done; however, until we can concentrate on them to the exclusion of everything else, we won't get it done."

"It's been hanging over our heads for wheat, now six generations?"

"And they just get stronger and they add more people, each more violent and rabid than before. They want to population of the earth to plummet because they think that only then will the earth come back into balance."

"I thought the earth was pretty good as it was?"

"According to them, we, that is, humans, are causing the problems to the ecosystem by our very existence and only our going into some new paradigm is going to fix that. The new paradigm is death, of course."

"Not good. Now that the war, excuse me, the police action, in Vietnam, is done and you kids' generation are settling into families and raising your own, we need to take the strain off of some of you so the next generation doesn't grow up shell shocked. Bad enough some of them have to live in town and not in the country. Especially that child of Noel's. What a boy! He's what? Five?"

"Four and a math whiz." smiled Noel. "We have some of our friends looking to tutor he and his sibs."

"You get that boys and his sibs what they need. Family will pay for it. Well, we need to get more eyes on this info. Not ready to release to the government yet; we need more data. Who can we assign that isn't?" As the planning went on, Noel leaned back in his chair and mused. *"Violet really doesn't like living in*

Washington. Wonder if I can move us out to the old farm in Arlington so the kids have more space? She's nearly done at OSU, and she loves her job at Children's Services. I still have eight years to get my twenty in at Special forces, and we can move then but the kids will be nearly teens. I wonder if...no Violet wouldn't go for that but it might be an option."

"Noel?"

"What?"

"Since you're still technically in the military, can you keep your eyes open on the ones listed as being in military Major White, Captain Davis?"

"Whoa. White got promoted?"

"Yeah, he got promoted. We're putting you over into his section ASAP . You did hear about your promotion?"

"No, guess not. I assumed they'd give me some sort of medal for getting shot again. I know I'm supposed to go back to Fort Bragg right after I leave here."

"You're the first Lieutenant in the newly minted MARCON group. It combines men from all ranks and branches of the military; sort of the best of the best. You'll get your first orders when you get to Bragg. You're going to be directly under Davis and White and keep your eyes open. Report back to Summermoon if you see anything odd. And watch your back."

"Violet's not going to be glad of this. I'd put in for being based at Anacostia so I could fly home more often."

"You're going to be sent there shortly, as is White. How is Violet?"

"With one kid a verified genius, one kid highly gifted and one almost normal, she's glad she can go to Lucas' place occasionally and work out frustrations. She hauls all the kids over and they play in the Zen garden with the masters who think they're darling-what do a bunch of confirmed bachelors know? Even after Kai buried a lollipop in the white sand garden...made it pretty sticky. He learned how to rake it clean that day."

"Not a bad thing. Is Violet upping skills we ought to know about?"

"She's nearly to her second black belt. She's building a network in her branch of the government. She's more occupied with the babies right now than anything."

"And she ought to be. Angelica, we're adding Noel to the team; we'll add someone from each of the offices in each base to it. We have to get to the bottom of the mess. And what about this Obsidian woman, Noel?" asked Glen.

"Obsidian?"

"She'd paid us a visit at the Colorado lab and tried to hire away some of the tribals for her own use? Seems she's starting a think tank on her own."

"Oh yeah, her. Lab ladies kicked her out, I hope?"

"She claimed she was real good friends with you during the war."

"Correct that to she tried, took a swing at me and Violet intercepted. She never made it to base."

"Good, she strikes me as a slimy sort. Works for a munitions group right now, sales or something like that, as a cover. She wanted some of our researchers."

"Rather you didn't tell Violet. She sort of threw her overboard last time she saw her, I mean literally. Right off the deck of the ship while we were on maneuvers. Had the awfullest time getting us out of that."

Glen smiled and then shook his head as he chuckled. "Yeah, heard about that from a colleague. Violet's feisty all right. Now on to the next business, Malcolm has a report from Jerome on the Continent.."

The meeting went on for another hour, reports and assignments. Finally they adjourned and went out to eat with the rest of the family and do what they could to relax before heading back to their homes.

Chapter 30

Busy productive years passed. Lilianna was born to Noel and Violet as Noel worked towards finishing his military career in the reserves and going full time into the family business. Violet had a solid network of colleagues. Having worked at the county and state level, she had been working in Washington for several years at Health and Human Services at the Federal level. She had published in several journals and guest taught at her old Alma Mater as well as other colleges. She was a well-accepted expert in childhood mental illness.

Noel was being groomed to take over from his father Glen who was approaching retirement age. Violet wanted to retire. She talked about retiring. She was expecting another child. But she hated to not be part of helping make the world better and she loved working with her husband. But summer break came for the children's schooling and with it the next hurdle to be crossed; summer camp.

"It's the best thing for our sons, Violet."

"But all summer? I'm to not see them all summer?"

"Gabriel and Kai will go to the Rez to live with Storyteller along with other young men of our tribe, They'll learn the traditions and make lifelong friends. Since Gabe is now seven, he's old enough to go. Kai should have gone last year but we wanted them to go together; you remember. They're to take care of each other."

"But all summer?"

"It's only twelve weeks, wife. And we can concentrate on Jasmine and Lilianna here. They don't go to girls camp until they're a little older."

"Why do the boys have to start so young?"

"They have to be warriors and parents don't do that training well, especially moms."

"But they've been taking marital arts from Lucas and they're tutored in math and languages."

"Wife, I know. They look little to us. To the trainers, they will look like young men and they will learn their place in warrior society. "

"And why can't I pack for them? When did the tribal elders-who are all men incidentally, make that decision?"

"Last summer, wife of my heart. Moms have a tendency to pack too many comforts. They are only allowed to bring the clothes they wear and a knife. I will give them each a knife this evening in ceremony and then they will leave."

"One outfit? For twelve weeks? They'll smell like monkeys and get skin rashes. I can't even ride there with them?"

"No, wife. You've been in the tribe since birth and I've not known you to fight a traditional thing so hard."

"This is not traditional. This is a recent development and I daresay none of the Mothers were included in the deliberations. Why the sudden change in age for boys' training?"

"Maybe not the way it has always been done, but these are extenuating times. Since the last two wars left many of our young men without the tools to fight and keep safe the men decided to train the warriors early in case this idiot government started another war our young men would have to attend. And you know, within our family firm we train our children early Our training has kept us alive more than once, having the skills learned from the elders. They will be safe. We will not lose so many men next war."

"The next war? Weren't the World wars and Korea and Vietnam enough for you men? Kai is going to be a scientist."

"He already is. My son's like a dry cloth on a wet ground, sucking up knowledge where ever he finds it."

"But little Gabe,"

"Is little no longer. He is seven and needs treated with responsibility. "

"He has such a gentle heart, always carrying things home to save."

"Yes, I know. He may be a great doctor one day. Right now, he needs to learn to walk before he flies." Standing up, he went to his study. It hurt to disagree with his wife of many years. She was a wise woman, a clan Mother, respected and intelligent and she just was thinking with her heart this time, not her head. He knew that but it didn't make it easier. He went in, closed the door and then went to his corner to pray for more wisdom.

After supper that night, Noel took his two sons into the back garden. Under the stars, he took out a knife and showed it to them.

"When I was your age, my father gave me this knife, which I have carried ever since. It has saved my life many times. It was made by the old flint knapper in our village. The handle is bone. The blade is steel. He told me to only use it to support my family or defend others, not in anger nor in hate. Now it is your turn to carry a knife and learn to be a warrior for our tribe and family." Noel bent and unwrapped two knives which had been rolled up in deerskin.

"These knives I had made for you by the same flint knapper that made my knife, old Brightfire. They may be too large for you to wield now, but you will carry them with you to the camp and you will learn how to care for them and

167

eventually how to use them. Listen carefully to what you are told. Learn all you can because the skills you learn over this summer will be vital to you later. I shall take you to the land tomorrow morning. We leave before dawn, so you need to get to bed soon." He handed Kai his knife in its' sheath. Kai seemed fascinated with the way it was made. Gabriel handed his knife back.

"I don't want a knife, Daddy. Mother says I'm not old enough to have a knife, not even a pocketknife. I am not going to make Mom mad."

"Your Mom knows you have it, and you will be careful."

Gabriel shook his head. "No, Daddy. Not yet. I don't want a knife until I know Mom's OK with me having it too." Kai looked at his brother and at the new knife in his hand. He shook his head. "Gabe's right, Daddy. You keep the knives for us. We'll get old enough for them soon enough. Besides, I might lose it climbing trees."

Noel considered his boys and took the knives. smiled. "It takes a smart man to know when he's not old enough for something." He gave his boys a hug. "You make me proud. Now off to bed with the both of you."

Violet was watching in the shadows and came out as the boys ran in. "I'm really very proud of them," she sniffed. "I just am going to miss them so."

"They'll be home. Twelve weeks will go fast. I saw you working out pretty hard this afternoon."

"I'm going to lose this baby fat if I die trying," she growled.

"I didn't see any baby fat."

"You're just being nice. I have ten pounds more to lose and by golly it's going."

"It's not like you're a magician's assistant, having to hide in tight places."

"Are you kidding? I'm the wife of an Oberllyn. I am always hiding in tight places. Now let's go tuck in the kids. Jasmine's down for the night and so is Lilianna."

"And we will be shortly as well."

Chapter 31

Storyteller and his friend Wildfox met the men at the lodge.

"Aho! Yoh nii joos! Are these the new braves I have heard about?"

"Here they are Grandfather," smiled Noel. "This is Kai, this Gabriel."

"We will have a naming ceremony for you when you have earned a new name. For now, these names will do," said Wild Fox. "Come and meet the other braves being trained this time. You will stay with them in a group." He led the two boys away from their father who watched them go and got in his car and drove away. *"Guess I'm not as tough as I thought," he muttered to himself. "Getting a little misty eyed myself. Hard to believe I've got kids old enough to go through warrior training already. I hope what they've learned from Lucas helps them. I hope what I've taught them helps them. I hope they grow strong in tradition and can take their place in the tribe and in the family. Father God, please be with my boys. And maybe keep us busy this summer so we don't dwell on missing them so much."*

Back at the camp, Wildfox led Kai and Gabriel to a small clearing under the trees where three other boys were learning to build a lean to from an older boy.

"Coyote, I have two more small ones for you to help settle in for the night. Boys, this is Coyote; he has been at camp three summers and is going to be your leader. This is Puma, Cougar, Windtalker and Beavertail. You will meet others of the tribe also training. Now, you need to take your knives and come over here so he can show you how to cut down some boughs to make a lean to with proper thankfulness."

Kai looked at his little brother. "We don't have knives. We aren't old enough."

"How are you going to build a lean to?" asked Coyote.

"Let me think." said Kai.

"I can loan you my knife," offered Cougar.

"Won't it hurt the trees if we cut off their limbs?" asked Gabriel.

"And isn't there a lodge?" asked Kai.

"Not for survival training."

"Do we have any twine or rope?"

"We use lashes made of the bark of trees." Kai looked around himself and turned slowly, studying.

"I think I know a way. Come on, Gabriel."

"No, Wait a minute! You can't go anywhere but here. We have to stay together." protested Cougar.

"We're still here. We aren't going anywhere except up," said Kai cheerfully. He and Gabe were twenty feet up in a tree by now. "This place here, you think?"

Gabriel nodded. "It will do unless there's a thunderstorm."

"Get down here! I can't let you fall out of a tree." Cougar was doing his best to sound authoritative, adult and in charge. He was losing that fast.

"We aren't falling. We're building a gorilla nest."

"You're what?"

"Gorillas build sleeping nests in trees at night for safety. This is a perfect spot. It doesn't harm the trees, it leaves little trace of where you've been. Lean to's can be seen and they take too much time."

"First," said Coyote quietly, in what he hoped sounded like an in control voice, "You aren't gorillas. Second, This is not Africa. We're natives in the middle of Ohio. Second, you

172

have to learn to build a lean to. You have no way to, what are you doing now?" He couldn't help it. His voice squeaked.

"We're weaving the branches together to make a floor."

"We want to build a tree house, too," complained Puma. "It looks like fun."

"It won't be fun if it rains and they get all soaked and cold," explained Coyote. "You two come down and I will let you use my knife to cut some branches off."

"Is there a problem?" asked Skinwalker as he walked up. "I just brought supplies in for the camp. Is that Kai up there? Hi, son!"

"They won't come down. They are supposed to be helping us build a lean to," puffed Coyote in frustration. "I can't decide whether they are foolish or stubborn or being deliberately disrespectful?"

"Have you asked them that?"

"Well, not exactly, but I'm supposed to teach them how to make shelter and they didn't bring knives so they decided to make gorilla nests,"

"Really?" asked Skinwalker. "I might take a fancy to one of those myself. I've built enough of them in the bush." He looked up and then started to shinny up the tree.

"Hi, boys," he said cheerfully. "Quite a drop down."

"We can use our belts to tie ourselves in if it makes you feel better," offered Kai. "There, that one is tight. Gabe?"

"Having some trouble with this branch. I'm not sure I'm strong enough to pull it and hold it securely."

"Boys, can you stop just a minute and listen to me?" they both looked up and sat back. "Coyote is just becoming a teacher this year. He's never had that much responsibility and you two are causing him unneeded pain."

"Really?" asked Kai, looking at Gabriel. "But since we didn't have knives he asked us to figure out how we were going to build shelter, and so we decided this would cause the woods

173

less damage than just trying to break off branches. This way, come morning, we just let them loose again. It doesn't take long to build. Da showed us how."

"Did you notice how Coyote was having them all build one lean to so you would all be in it and so you could share the warmth of the fire and each other? No one would have to be alone in the dark that way." Kai leaned over. The other boys were hauling more branches over to the pile of branches.

"I thought they were each building their own lean to."

"It may have appeared that way, but you need to cut Coyote some slack."

"But we didn't bring knives. Mom wasn't ready for us to have knives." explained Kai. "She was afraid we'd get hurt and she didn't want us to come in the first place."

"I didn't want to come either," said Gabriel. "I miss mom. And I think the woods at night is scary. Up here at least nothing can get to us. When we were at Bear feast some of the other boys told me that the older kids like to scare the younger ones and I should be ready for them to come running through the camp pretending to be Bigfoot or a bear or something. I don't like being scared. I don't like to hurt people. It' safer up here than down there. I wish mom was here."

"It's good for you to love and obey your Mother," replied Skinwalker slowly. "But it's good to learn to work with others. And if someone were so foolish as to try and run through warriors' camp in the dark, I think we can set up some surprises to stop them. In the meantime, if you don't have a knife, I can let you use my wire. It works."

"Wire?"

"You need to come down and I'll show you." Kai looked at Gabriel. "We'd better unweave things. We'd not like to harm one of the trees." They quickly unwove the branches and skimmed down the trunk. Skinwalker took them over to a small tree two of the others were trying to hack down for the middle support of the lean to and not having much success.

"It sure is hard with just a pocketknife," complained Beavertail.

"I suppose it is." said Skinwalker. "Allow me, gentlemen." He took a long coiled wire out of his pocket and wrapped it around the tree. Moving quickly, he used it to saw through the little tree trunk, working it back and forth. "Back up guys, let it fall, then let's get it over there."

"That's neat!" exclaimed Kai. "May I see it?"

"For a moment."

Kai studied the cutting wire and then handed it back carefully wound into a circle. " Kai, what can you see that you can do to help without a knife?" Kai looked up. He saw another boy struggling to pull a large branch over.

"I could help move things."

"Yes. What else?"

"We could help stack things?"

"Good. It's important for all warriors to help one another. Now go." Kai and Gabriel helped pull the tree over and listened to Coyote explain how the hut all went together so as to shed water and keep them warm and did not interrupt even when Kai felt Cougar was being dogmatic about how the boughs should be placed. Working together, in a couple hours, they had a serviceable shelter.

Coyote moved on to how to find dry kindling and firewood and they stacked it under the edges of the lean-to, then using softer branches piled inside made beds. They each stretched a blanket over the piles.

That night, they went to the lodge to eat. Storyteller took them out to the center campfire and told them the first of many tales they would hear that summer.

"Kunakwat, lowat, nuchink, this is how all tales begin among our people. Say it together? Kunakwat, lowat, nuchink.

175

Many long moons ago, when the Munsee and other Delaware people lived in the East, before the great move away from our first homes by the Big waters, a Delaware man and his wife went on a long hunt quite a ways from the village. They had been out several days without having any luck when one night as they were sitting around their camp fire an owl hooted from a tree nearby and after hooting laughed. This was considered a good omen, but to make sure of this the hunter took a chunk of fire and retired a little way from the camp under the tree where the owl was perched, and laid the chunk of fire on the ground, and sitting by it began to sprinkle tobacco on the live coal and talk to the owl. He said: "Mo-hoo-mus (or Grandfather), I have heard you whoop and laugh. I know by this that you see good luck coming to me after these few days of discouragement. I know that you are very fond of the fat of the deer and that you can exercise influence over the game if you will. I want you to bring much game in my way, not only deer, but fur-bearing animals, so that I may return home with a bountiful supply of furs as well as much dried meat, and I will promise you that from the largest deer that I kill, I will give you the fat and heart, of which you are very fond. I will hang them in a tree so that you can get them." The owl laughed again and the hunter knew that he would get much game after that.

The next morning he arose early, just before day, and started out with his bow and arrow, leaving his wife to take care of the camp. He had not gone far before he killed a very large buck. In his haste to take the deer back to camp so that he could go out and kill another before it got too late, he forgot his promise to the owl and did not take out the fat and heart and hang it in the tree as he said he would do, but flung the deer across his shoulder and started for camp. The deer was very heavy and he could not carry it all the way to camp without stopping to rest. He had only gone a few steps when he heard the owl hoot. This time it did not laugh as it had the night before.

The owl flew low down, right in front of the man, and said to him: "Is this the way you keep your promise to me? For this falsehood I will curse you. When you lay down this deer, you will fall dead." The hunter was quick to reply: "Grandfather, it is true I did not hang the fat up for you where I killed the deer, but I did not intend to keep it from you as you accuse me. I too have power and I say to you that when you alight, you too will fall dead. We will see who is the stronger and who first will die." The owl made a circle or two and began to get very tired, for owls can only fly a short distance. When it came back again, it said: "My good hunter, I will recall my curse and help you all I can, if you will recall yours, and we will be friends after this." The hunter was glad enough to agree, as he was getting very tired too. So the hunter lay the deer down and took out the fat and the heart and hung them up. When he picked up the deer again it was much lighter and he carried it to his camp with perfect ease. His wife was very glad to see him bringing in game. She soon dressed the deer and cut up strips of the best meat and hung them up to dry, and the hunter went out again and soon returned with other game.

In a few days they had all the furs and dried meat they could both carry to their home, and the hunter learned a lesson on this trip that he never afterwards forgot, that whenever a promise is made it should always be fulfilled. Just so you , children, when you make a promise, you should always do all in your power to keep it. Your word is your most precious possession and you need to carry it carefully as any other possession. Aho! My tale is done! "

Kai and Gabriel felt their eyes get heavy as he spoke. Shortly, they were dismissed to go back to their lean-to where they found that while they were gone, someone had come and left them some provisions for the next morning.

177

"In the morning, we will learn to make fire and cook our breakfast. We gather at night to receive tradition from the elders, but during the day, we learn."

Puma bumped Kai. "I'm glad you decided not to stay up in the tree."

"Skinwalker is pretty persuasive." Kai replied. "He pointed out an error in my thinking."

"You talk different, " said Beavertail.

"I do?"

"More like a grownup. Hey, Gabriel, is he putting this on?"

"No, he pretty much talks like that at home too. At least it's in English. Jasmine is already learning French and she's pretty miserable to try and understand. Liliana just gurgles a lot and gets into my stuff."

"Your mom and Da are pretty famous." remarked Puma.

"Really? Why?" asked Gabriel.

"Your Da is sort of the head of a big army thing. He's a spy and stuff like Skinwalker."

Gabriel looked at Kai. "What's a spy?" he asked.

"It's when Da goes off on those trips for the military to get intel."

"What's intel?" asked Beavertail, yawning.

"I don't have the faintest idea." replied Kai. "I just know it's good. Da gathers it a lot. I suspect it's a vegetable. Grownups like vegetables."

Coyote sighed. "Guys, it's been a long day. Let's sleep."

Chapter 32

"That's quite a promotion, wife," remarked Noel as he snuggled with his wife in their big four poster bed. "Very proud of you."

"It means I have to leave the farm here and move to Washington. Not so fond of that. Can you get a transfer to Washington?"

"We could stay at Arlington."

"I know, but Summermoon's family is there now and I'd not feel right taking over and as many of us as there are, we would. We can rent something near the capitol. Sure going to miss the local folks. Can't imagine how I ended up in the Washington bureau. I figured the state level was as high as I'd go."

"You forget all those scholarly things you published, and all those seminars and how you were able to increase services while lowering budgets without losing personnel. Even bureaucrats are going to notice stuff like that."

"I guess so. Wish the kids weren't so small. Serena is such a bright little angel."

"She sure was cute riding yesterday. Does well at that. In Washington, we'll be closer to Lucas' Motherhouse and they can take studies there."

"Yes, that's right. What do your folks think about it all?"

"Well, I've only a few more years to complete the military I agreed to do and when I do, Da's going to retire to California. Not that he won't keep his hand in, just not as active."

The phone by the bed rang. Noel reached over and picked it up.

"Yes? What. You are kidding, right? This isn't a joke. Oh, my lord. Yes, we'll get up and go right now. Sending someone? Good. I'll meet you at the office."

"What? It's two in the morning."

"Something awful is about to take place. Glen needs me now. He has people coming to take the kids in custody and put them at Lucas place for safety's sake."

"What on earth is it?"

"We have to try and prevent something happening. We probably won't be able to. Stay with Lucas. I'll be home when I can. I have to fly to Washington."

Violet ran from room to room, grabbing the children' emergency bags, waking them up, apologizing, putting night coats over their pj's and pushing them to the front door to stand by their bags. She yanked on her own clothes and stacked her bag by the front door. Noel gave her a quick kiss and was out the front door just as two of Sensai Lucas' men stepped in. They grabbed the bags by the door and raced them to a car, then came and helped carry children out. The door was locked, the alarm set and the cars pulled out in the midnight darkness.

"Mommy, what's going on?" asked Jasmine. "I was in such a beautiful dream." She yawned.

"Your Da is headed to help his da in Washington. There's some trouble. We're going to stay at Lucas' house for a while with his kids."

"That will be great," enthused Kai. "Me and Ling ho"

"Ling ho and I,"

"OK, Ling ho and I, can hang out in the barn and practice holds."

"You might be able to do that eventually but I think we're going into lock-down."

Kai eyes got large. "What's lock down?" asked Gabriel.

"It means we're staying in the basement shelter. It's such a cool place. We're only allowed there during emergencies. Something bad must have happened. Last time was that tornado."

"Are we having one of those again?" asked Gabriel looking out the window in the dark.

"No, we are not," replied his Mother. "But after this is over, we might wish it so."

Chapter 33

Noel drove to the military airport and was rushed to a helicopter. He left immediately. In the vehicle with him was Wildfox and Skinwalker.

"What's going on?"

"Jerome's on his way in from Canada. There's going to be an attack."

"On American soil? Are you out of your mind? I thought we'd been able to diffuse that."

Skinwalker shook his head. "Just because we're here does not make us immune. Family safe?"

"With Lucas."

"Mine is as well. Here's what I know so far."

Over the racket of the chopper, the three men huddled around a laptop, reading communiques, gasping, shaking their heads. They made it to Washington and were met by cars to take them to Headquarters.

"Where's Glen?" asked Noel as he entered the bunker like building outside the capitol.

"He's at the Pentagon coordinating. We think the target's in New York. We aren't sure when, today sometime. Several targets."

"What are the sources?"

"Believe it or now, social media, the Dark Web, terrorists sites all bragging about what's happening today will bring the US to its knees, the usual garbage, but then suddenly silence; just all dead. You heard about Massoud? Massoud was assassinated by al-Qaeda yesterday. Scuttlebutt was because he tried to warn us there was an attack coming by air. Rice and Rumsfeld we thought had cleared all that as bragging among thieves, so to speak, but with the assassinations and the sudden silence and this other stuff, we got bad feelings going on. The Israeli Mossad has been passing along intel, as has Pakistan. It's giving us an uncomfortable picture. We've got the President out of the White house for a few days on tour and his Security detail has been pumped up. We're pretty sure it's going down today sometime, somewhere but we have to figure out the targets."

"Well, if this is right, we only have a few hours."

Summermoon nodded. "And we need to eliminate all but four targets from this list in time to evacuate them all to lessen the loss of life."

"Well, the terrorists themselves have people in the World Trade center, so probably wouldn't hit that. They could try the White House or Pentagon but surely they'd know about the protections in place there, and the United Nations seems to be on their side so why bomb them?" mused Skinwalker.

"Can't eliminate based on our preconceived notions. Let's crunch some facts. White House needs updates on progress every half hour; Glen wants it every fifteen minutes. Start crunching."

Nodding to Summermoon, the men sat at their terminals in the bunker collecting data, compiling ideas, clearing assumptions, making probable eliminations. Three hours later, seven thirty, they sent their final best guess for targets and personnel to the President, to Glen and to intelligence agencies around the country; including copies to their own network around the globe.

"We've done what we can. As long as they don't attack for a few more hours, we ought to be able to protect at least human lives."

"This is going to really hurt Wall Street." remarked Wildfox, sitting back. "Jerome's talking to the President from the sit room right now."

"It's going to hurt the world economy if it goes down." replied Skinwalker. "Glad my money's in land and alpaca."

"Is there anyone else to call?" Noel asked.

"Da said to just keep checking and trying to figure out who the guys are," remarked Summermoon. "He thinks we may have gotten it in time. If Glen can convince them to close those buildings and evacuate personnel, we ought to be able to stop loss of life at least. We need to keep working and refining."

"I'm for just a bite to eat first. There's sandwiches in the fridge and we just sent out the last intel to Glen. They're running it through the Pentagon staff now. We can start over and go over it again when we've had a sandwich. Otherwise we could start making dumb mistakes."

"I'm with that. Let's go." the men got up and stretched and headed over to the kitchenette.

"Besides, we've figured out that it's al-Qaeda. We've got that down. And some clown named Bin Laden. That's not going to change in the time it takes me to hog down a grinder." Skinwalker scratched his head as he took a submarine sandwich from the tray Summermoon sat on the counter. "Thanks for the coffee."

"Is this going to harm relations with the Saudi's?" asked Noel.

"He's Saudi but we can't blame them." replied Wildfox.

"Why not? If this list is correct the majority of people on it are Saudi."

"Just like the Hell's Angels and the Bloods are US citizens-does not make them good citizens. Just cause Al-Qaeda is Saudi doesn't make all Saudi's bad. We're dealing with fanatics here."

"Guess you're right."

"Think we'll be asked to locate Bin Laden?"

"Don't know that I'd want that assignment. Marcon might get it. He has to be stopped if he tries this trick."

Summermoon, eating and monitoring the news networks suddenly interrupted.

"Guys, you need to tune into CNN."

"What?"

"It's going down now. They did not, repeat, did not evacuate."

"What?"

"No one was warned."

"But they were given the intel. They had reasonable proof of danger. They couldn't have not believed it. They had time to move."

"Belief is not what's in question. Efficiency is-they got the intel but then had to process it themselves, oh, no. They just got the World trade center." Watching in horror, the events of the day rapidly spun out of control. The Twin Towers fell. The Pentagon was hit. The White House was only safe due to the actions of some brave men on the plane. The President sat in a classroom of children looking stunned.

Glen had been killed in the Pentagon attack. Several family members had been stationed at the World Trade center and helped folks out but were lost themselves.

Back home, the families of the Oberllyn's sat in stunned silence as the reports came through. A memorial service was held for Glen and the other firm members who died in the attacks. Jerome, by family assent, came out of retirement and took over the head of the firm temporarily until Noel could complete his military commitment. The entire country was in shock for several months, but then life took over, people shook themselves, and life went on.

Chapter 34

Noel was transferred to the Pentagon a year after that, and Violet did well at her post at Health and Human Services. She constantly networked, traveling up the ladder in the agency. The children grew and in 2010, the family reunion in California was a happy, noisy one. The children's names were all added to the family tree. The food was wonderful and the Ancient Oak still stood.

Jerome stood at the table and smiled.

"As is our custom, after we have added all the new faces and names, we remember those who have gone before us. Our beloved leader and father, friend, husband, brother, Glen, killed at the Pentagon September 11, 2001, along with Michael, Samuel, Angela and Martin. Glen's daughter Lacey Mystfawn came and lived with the wife and I after her Mother passed and now has completed her formal studies at Cambridge and works for us under David Skinwalker in the British branch of the service. Glen's wife passed quietly five years ago and walks the Skylands with Glen and all the other members of our family. Theodore Wildfox died in his sleep after a long life of service two years ago. Noel has finally completed his military service and will be taking over this firm so I can go retire at long last. Folks, I am 76; be real. I am retiring. I was never meant to be a leader, just a scientist. I want to enjoy my final years. As far as other accomplishments within the family, Kai has finished his undergraduate work and is joined at Stanford by my son Skinwalker. Kai's fifteen now, and nothing will hold that child back. I hate to think what he's going to do to my old alma mater. Cougar and Beavertail are going to MIT, Coyote Red has gone into law, which is totally not what we expected; however he's going to Harvard so the boy's not doing too bad. Gabriel finished his eagle scout badge by helping some beavers rebuild a dam that had been busted up by vandals when he visited me this summer in Maine. Violet has just been appointed to assistant Secretary of HHES in Washington. Jasmine won an award, first place actually, at the state horsemanship convention in Columbus. We've had six babies born, two weddings this last decade. The last decade has been good to our family in spite of some of the pain. Our investments have done well and out network grows and we have been able to be a force of good in the world; we were able to stop some evil. We were unable to stop other things. We built a new lab in New Zealand; we grew the labs in Scotland, Texas and South America. We still search for the elusive Brotherhood discovered in the last century. It appears to have morphed into something even darker and more sinister; it has allied itself with loose terrorist groups and is funding some of them, money laundering for others. It is heavily into the slave trade worldwide.. We still battle terrorism. We still look for the future. And may the Good Lord and Creator, who creates with a thought, be with us all in the next decade as he has been with us always in the past." He closed the book and smiled. "And now I'm ready for some food. Anyone with me?"

Chapter 35

Violet spoke to Noel.

"Noel, I'm going to go over to Storyteller's house for a few days. I need to walk the land."

"Is there something bothering you, wife?"

"I can't put my finger on it, and since there's a lull in the local politicking for summer, it's a good time. Can you hold down the fort?"

"If I can't after all these years, I'm ready for replacement."

She smiled and hugged her husband. "They've been good years. I'll see you by the weekend."

"Do you good to get out of the city." She nodded and went to pack.

"Odd," thought Noel. "Last time she got moody like that she was pregnant with Serena. We're too old for another child? Could have sworn we did the hot flash thing a couple years ago. Hate to think all that turmoil was just job stress. Father, have you and she been hiding something from me?" Violet landed in Columbus Airport and rented a small car. Violet sped along the highway heading for the land. It was a two hour trip from the airport and she looked forward to talking to the elders about the coming Harvest festival among other things.

Pulling into the long driveway leading back to Storyteller's house, she looked at the signs of fall, the changing colors on the leaves, the animals with winter coats, the intense blue of the sky between the golden and red leaves and sighed.

"I think a couple good walks and talks with the elders will set my mind at ease. I wonder if Mother Whitetail is about?" she pulled to a stop at the parking area and walked downhill the rest of the way, breathing in the quiet. Halfway there, a woman stepped out of the forest. "Whitetail! I was thinking about you!" said Violet.

"I had a dream last night about you coming soon. I am glad to see I was right," she smiled. "I was just gathering some things before the cold set in and these old bones would complain too much for a long walk."

"Can I help you carry anything?"

"No, but it appears to me you're carrying something."

Violet shook her head. "I'm not ready yet to talk about it all."

"Well, Storyteller and I are here when you're ready."

"I think maybe a walk and maybe a sweat lodge would help get me ready."

"Then bring your bag down to the lodge. The sweat lodge has been waiting since morning for you."

"What?"

"Old Storyteller got up this morning and started up the fire, and filled the water barrel. The rocks are heated and waiting. He said he just felt in his bones it would be needed. I can attend you, me and Singing Wind. She's here. I'll just go get some things."

Violet sat her purse and her bag on the front porch of the lodge.

"Aho, sister, I greet you," said a quiet voice.

"Storyteller! So glad to be here."

"Washington is not a good place these days?"

"I hate it more each day. So much confusion, so loud. And I have so many decisions to make."

"Decisions are not bad in themselves, but I think you need quiet."

"I do."

"Then let's put your things in the sleeping area. You go down to the Sweat Lodge. The women will attend you there."

Violet went inside, changed into a swim suit, put a wrap on and walked the path to the sweat lodge, stilling her mind by concentrating on the sounds around her; birds, a squirrel arguing with the wind, leaves starting to fall, branches rubbing. She got to the sweat lodge, accepted a glass of warm meadow tea and went inside. The door was closed. She tied a prayer tie to the ones already hanging on the walls. Then she poured cool water on the heated rocks and the steam rose up with a hiss like a hot spring. She sat back, relaxed her muscles and began a soft prayer.

Outside, the Nation's Mother and clan Mother sat quietly and watched. Storyteller, in the distance, shook his rattle and chanted. Inside, in the dark and steam and quiet, Violet laid her hands across her belly and sighed as she felt the baby kick for the first time. She smiled to herself and she prayed to Creator for this last child to come.

"I thought I was too old for this blessing," she prayed. "I just hope this little one will be fine. I am really too old."

She added water to the stones. The women outside lifted the flap and added more heated rocks to the pile. The temperature was intense and Violet poured some water over her shoulders. She sat a while longer, and then left the heat of the lodge and ran down to the pond below her where she dove in. Swimming to the bottom of the autumn cooled spring water, she grabbed a handful of the bottom silt and swam back up. When she got back to the shore, she looked at what she had.

The Nation's Mother came over to her with a towel.

"Here, you are, dear," she said quietly. "What did you do?"

"Oh, I was just thinking of the old tradition that says if you grab some pebbles from the bottom of the pond it will give you some insight into what's going to happen."

"You mean trying to figure out the sex of your child?"

"How did you know?"

"It's why I didn't allow you to stay in the lodge longer. Not good for older moms to sweat that much. What did you find?"

"One of those little cores from making beads, and a white stone and a sort of red one. I think quartz and maybe flint?"

"And what do you think it tells you?"

"I didn't dig deep enough?"

Nation's Mother laughed. "No, the bead core shows he will live traditional. Flint is the sign of a warrior and quartz of a wise person. So your son will be wise, and traditional." She frowned a moment. "And as far as it goes, that seems right."

"As far as it goes?"

"Toss the stones back and come up for some tea. Storyteller may have something to add."

Violet and her friends walked up, talking about the approaching festival, the tribal news. Violet went in and got into warm dry clothes, came down and accepted a cup of tea.

She sat down in front of the fireplace.

"That feels good. I feel tired but relaxed."

Storyteller nodded. "Yes, relaxed is good. Sister, we have been troubled in our souls about your child."

"Did everyone know about this baby but my husband and me? I am sort of old for a child."

"I think he has guessed. But this child will be different from any of your other children. He will be distant."

"Distant?"

"He will be intelligent like Kai, gentle like Gabriel, curious like Jasmine, love animals like Serena, analytical like Noel and wise, like yourself, but you will not see it until much

192

later. You must work with him, you must love him. One like him seldom comes to our people and when they do grace us, they must be raised with care. Always they have ended up leaders. His mind will travel elsewhere even when awake."

"That's a lot to take in. But distant?"

"From an infant, you will search for him, for his soul. You will bring it back from wandering. It is not firmly with him."

"His soul wanders?"

"It does. You must help him settle to earth and to bond to his family. He will never bond firmly to this earth so you must bind him firmly to your family and to the tribe. It will keep him centered."

"I still don't understand."

"As you time grows closer, you will begin to. It is only after he is born that it will be clear. Do not be discouraged. It will be clear what his purpose is as he grows."

They sat in silence as Violet considered the elders words. Finally, Whitetail asked them to come to supper. They talked again of the harvest festival and tribal happenings, good gossip-who's child had excelled, who was expecting. Finally, Violet went to bed and slept better than she had in years.

The next morning, Violet took along walk, helped around the lodge to make preparations for the feast to come. She sewed on a quilt to be gifted a young couple who were getting married at the Festival, and cut out some baby moccasins for some infants who were to be adopted. Finally after another day of resting, she packed up and headed back to the airport. Her flight left at 2; she was home by five that Friday night, feeling more refreshed than she had been in a long time.

As she snuggled up to Noel at bedtime, she explained that one last time they were going to be parents. She didn't tell him about the elder's warnings and advice. She just considered how to lower her workload a little so she'd have time to make this baby, her last one to be, a quilt and a soft baby blanket. She wondered what his older sibs would think. And she decided it was time to go talk to the obstetrician one last time. As she snuggled down to sleep, she smiled to herself. *I feel a little bit like Sarah, a little old for this but I think this time, I'm going to enjoy the whole process, knowing it's the last. I will absolutely not have anymore. Six is plenty. I wonder how I can squeeze a nursery out of the brownstone? Maybe since Kai is pretty well out, no, I think I need to move to a bigger place. And considering the situation in Washington, I need it to be better secured. I'll talk to Noel in the morning. I wonder if this child is going to be healthy? No, the elders said he would be, but older moms are more prone to Down's children. Maybe that's what Storyteller meant. No, not if he's as smart as Kai. I guess time will figure it out. But we do need to move.*

The family did move into a larger brownstone in Washington. They arranged for a specially trained nanny to be with the children as Violet worked. Her doctor told her that considering she was over forty, this was going to be a high risk baby and insisted she rest more, so she set up to do work at home and keep her feet up as the months progressed.

One day, Summermoon called her from Washington.

"I've got some sad news to relate," she said. "Jerome passed in his sleep last night."

"That's too bad. He was right then to retire when he did. At least he and his wife had a couple good years before he passed."

"His wife said his passing was easy, a good passing, he told her good bye and to always be true to God and family and herself. Her daughter is moving to her house to help her not be lonely. She'd finished college and was going to come work in the firm, but right now her mom needs her more."

"Iris always was such a good kid. She'll take good care of her mom."

"And mom now wants to go back to work to pass time, so we're setting up an office in her home and giving her some analysis to work on; Iris will help with it. They requested no funeral; they're having the burial there on his property in Maine. Iris said the family is so scattered, it's so hard to bring us together; if we would just all at noon tomorrow take a moment to pray for his family, he would appreciate it."

"Jerome was always such a private man."

"I don't think he ever quite recovered from the loss of his son."

"No, probably not. How is Skinwalker?"

"He's with the family. How have you been?"

"Well, Seven months along and I feel like a whale."

"Two months to go. You'll make it."

"I thought we were done when Serena came."

"How are the kids taking it?

"Kai's bemused and did a study on older moms and babies and the tendency to spoil the baby."

"That is so Kai!"

"Isn't it? And Gabriel wants to be at the delivery. Jasmine keeps checking my mental health to see if I've lost it yet. Last night she asked if she could use my mental health as a science project in coping skills. Lilianna says I ought to have used protection and it's not sharing her room, and Serena just sucks her thumb and snuggles against my belly. They're only going to be 18 months apart."

"So pretty much the same normal chaos?"

"Yes. Noel is trying not to be sent overseas anytime soon but there's 42 wars going on at any one time and he's just getting into his position. His contacts have stood him in good stead but even he can see the veracity in just retiring."

"Tell him it gets better. Since my hubby has cancer, I'm taking an extended leave to take care of him and the kids."

"We'll keep him in prayer and the rest as well."

"And we'll do the same and keep in touch."

Violet hung up, went into the kitchen to grab some lunch and saw Noel sitting there, just sitting, no laptop, no visible motion, just sitting.

"Noel?"

He looked at her. "Just practicing being in the moment Lucas says I do it poorly."

"I think you're so in the moment that you can't breathe."

"I was thinking the same thing. there's a lot to be said for being occupied. How's my wife?"

"She's fine. Junior kicks a lot."

"The doctor still insisting it's a girl?"

"Yes, and the elders insist it's a boy."

"Is it maybe, twins?"

"Or perhaps two spirits? I don't think know. I think he's something else. Anyway, I had the men paint the nursery lavender. I hung white and purple curtains and it's really cute You want to come see?"

"Actually, I want a sandwich. Then I'll look at the nursery."

His pager rang. "Blast it."

"Let me get the sandwich." she bustled around as he went to the phone and spoke quietly.

"OK, I am learning to delegate," he said. "Not everything needs my immediate response. where's my lunch?"

"Here it is, tomato, spinach, stripples, cheese, cashew nuts, and bread and butter pickles on sourdough rye." she shuddered. "How you ever are going to eat that combination. just can't understand how you invented that one."

"It's got the four food groups all in one sandwich. All need are three Oreo cookies and a glass of juice and I've got a complete meal."

"Have you even got taste buds?"

"Never really needed them. Besides, on maneuvers when you got to eat mealworms, it's helpful to not be squeamish."

"Noel! I mean ugh. I'm pregnant and unless you want to be cleaning up what's going to come up,"

"Ok, Ok, nuff said." He hugged his wife. "Let me finish, I'll check out that nursery, and you promise not to go into labor before I get back."

"Get back?"

"Lab said something about finding some of old Tesla's work in a file."

"Really? He was one of great Grandpa Noah's friends, wasn't he?"

"Yes, they had some doings. Filed away in a basement we found his papers. Before donating them to the Smithsonian, we're scanning them in for future reference. Some of its pretty interesting. Nothing we could use nowadays, but it was amazing for its' time. Edison's' stuff was all patented and it's pretty open, but Tesla didn't go that route, so a lot of this has never really been seen."

"How did we end up with them?"

"It appears that at some point, the old folks had to steal them back from spies of Edison's who were working with the Brotherhood to use."

"Wow! This goes that far back?"

"I know. It boggles me to see how things that happened before influence what happens to the now. Which brings me to Lucas suggestion to try and be more in the now. I don't see how to do that. I'll keep trying but the ancestors call me back."

Noel went and looked at the nursery, helped rearrange the furniture, checked that the security windows were indeed on, made sure the old rocking chair that Violet inherited from her Mother, and which had rocked all the babies on her side of the family, was indeed still sturdy, then hugged his wife one more time and left for the office.

Chapter 36

"Here's the most interesting design so far." said Alex, one of the scientists at the lab. "He shows what he called a death ray. It's an early version of laser."

"How on earth did he get a laser with the things available back then?"

"I'm not sure he did, but it was evidently an idea he was promoting as a way to cut ships in half. Sam actually built a prototype and the thing does laze and it does cut through wood. It wouldn't be strong enough for steel, but ships back in those days weren't primarily steel. Here's the infamous death ray, which he called peace ray, supposed to be able to bring down airplanes at 250 miles away to stop attacks. And here is an ozone generator, and here's a steam powered mechanical oscillator for causing earthquakes, ostensibly to make avalanches occur at more convenient times."

"We do that today to bring the danger down."

"Not using this, but had it been built, it would have worked, I think. Here are several others but this is the thing that caught my eye."

"It's not a machine at all?"

"No, it's notes he took of some meetings of a clandestine group called the Black Hand. They had approached him with requests he help design ' an electricity powered hydrogen filled airship'. He did design such a thing, but he didn't give them the plans. It appears this is a journal of his meetings with them. He mentions our ancestors in it, and how they helped him recover some things that had been stolen. He gave the rest of these plans to different governments but I don't think anyone actually worked on them that I can see. He was way ahead of his time."

"Wonder if we can correlate his journal with the family records?

"Already done. His notes and our journals match, so these were rescued by our folks. He never asked for them back probably figured his own life would be safer if he didn't have possession. So we ended up storing all this stuff."

"Amazing. So we're copying it all and then the plan is to give it to the Smithsonian?"

"That's the plan. Odd thing though. we've been contacted by someone from the Menlo Park museum about allowing them to display some of them there since they worked together for a while."

"I heard more like they had a private war together. Wouldn't it be odd if this helped bridge that? But I think the Smithsonian can decide who displays what. Let's just hand it off to them after copying it into archives."

"Will do."

"How long will it take to scab this all in?"

"I'm nearly done. Rest the afternoon and if you want to take it over then and formally hand it over to the museum, that would be fine."

"I'll set up a time for that. I enjoy talking to the folks there."

Chapter 37

Violet and Noel's son was born in October. He was sweet, chubby and had lots of dark hair with shiny white hairs interspersed as though he was a much older man. He seemed fine at first, but as time went on, he cried and would not be comforted unless swaddled. His eyes focused but would not look at people. He always seemed to be looking beyond others to study what was around. He would not make eye contact; he didn't respond to attention or smile or wave bye. Getting more and more worried, the pediatrician referred them to an expert on childhood development who studied little Micah and after a few tests and several hours of observation, told Violet and Noel that their son was autistic.

"It's not exactly a death sentence," she told the stunned parents. "There is a lot the family can do to alleviate symptoms. Be consistent. Keep to a regular schedule, reward behaviors that appear to be the child reaching out. I'm referring you to an autism clinic to enroll little Micah in. For now, love this child, talk to him, read to him, make a safe quiet zone for him in your home for him to retreat to, but don't allow him to completely withdraw. In many cases, with early interventions, many of the symptoms can be worked around, coped with and even extinguished."

On the drive home, Violet watched her son as Noel drove. Neither had much to say but were thinking over what had been told to them. Violet kept trying to get the baby to watch her fingers in front of his face. Baby Micah studied passing shadows on the roof of the car.

"Violet, the elders knew this baby would be different."

"They did."

"But they said he would be a leader."

"They did."

"And Storyteller called me before he was born and told me I would need to be strong, give this child more attention."

"I know."

"Violet, you didn't tell me any of this? What are you thinking?"

"That you are busy and worried about many things and this was going to mostly fall on me, so we would take one day at a time until we found out how big the problem was going to be. Now I'm thinking what we need to do. I'm thinking how this is going to be our most precious baby. And also that the entire family needs to be in on the cure, or adjustment or whatever."

"Lilianna was kind of right this morning."

"She said he was demented. Autism is not demented."

"No, but she knows he's different."

"Different is not bad. Watch out!" Violet had looked out just in time to see a red car T-bone their van. They were pushed across the street into a light pole that fell over on them. Both Violet and Noel had instinctively leaned over the baby, Noel grabbing Violet. The car alarm blared. A man got out of the red car, walking over to their car. He had a gun in his hand which he raised as he walked forward.

A shot rang out but was deflected from the car back at the shooter, who was hit in the leg. He tried to stand again, but someone in the crowd kicked his gun out of his hand. Noel shook his head, checked his wife and unable to open his door used a hammer to break out the windshield. Violet called for help, disconnected the baby seat and they crawled out of the vehicle.

Violet, holding the car seat, stumbled over to a corner store doorway and sat down. Micah made no sound. He started at the neon sign in the window, fascinated.

Noel went to where the shooter was trying to pull himself up.

"Who are you and why did you try to kill us?" he demanded.

"Long live the Black Hand!" the man said. Then he spit at Noel.

"The Black Hand's been disbanded for fifty years. Who are you really?"

"You think you're so smart, you Oberllyns." The siren was getting closer. "I'm worth nothing, but she is all."

"She?"

"You know nothing. Hail Gaia!" He pulled his sleeve back and flicked out a blade that had been tied to his wrist. Noel's reaction was automatic to try and disarm him, but the man didn't try to stab Noel. Instead, he turned the knife on his own neck and yanked it across. Noel tried to staunch the blood as the ambulance spun to a stop. The EMTs took over. Policemen rushed to speak to him.

"My wife, she's over there. This man tried to kill us." said Noel. "Please, can we go to my wife and baby?"

"Looks like the EMT's are over there with her and the baby. Do you have ID on you?"

"My name is Noel Oberllyn. My hands are sort of bloody but if you want to pull my wallet out of my back left pocket, along with my CCW, you can check it out." Noel turned around. The policeman pulled out the wallet, looked at the ID and said.

"Ok, then. Let's go over by your wife. Men, fan out, get witness statements. Any idea who the guy was that attacked your family?"

"I have no idea. I hope he survives to be interrogated. That's one I'd like to sit in on."

"Cut his own throat? Suicidal I suspect. Or a terrorist. Mrs. Oberllyn?"

Violet was quickly recovering. The medics checked her over and other than a bump and a few bruises, she seemed fine. They asked she and the baby, all of them to come in and be checked at the ER. Noel looked at them and shook his head.

"Wife, I know the baby was in his seat but he may not react as normal kids do and we'd not know if he was hurt. Let's go. "

"I need to call home. My purse is in the car and we'll need it at the hospital."

"I'll get it and while meet up with you at the ER," said the policeman. "We'll need statements."

"And we need answers," Noel nodded grimly as he entered the ambulance with his wife and child.

Chapter 38

"Really? The Black Hand? Gaia? What the heck!" declared Summermoon. "That's got to be the craziest thing I've ever heard."

"He's covering." replied Noel.

"Obvious. But he did succeed in dying before he could say more. What were they hoping to achieve by a suicide attack?"

"Prints on his weapons indicate he was an ex- inmate and a member of several clubs, worked as a night attendant at a convenience store, no family, named Jake Robbins. He has recently marched in several environmental type protests. He has a pretty regular schedule to his life. No one would suspect him of anything."

"What kind of message is that and from whom?" mused Skinwalker on the conference call.

"Don't know. Wait, I've got a call coming in from a detective down at the precinct. Noel Oberllyn. Hello, Bob."

"Noel, you wanted me to let you know if we found anything out. We've bumped this up to Homeland Security due to what we found at this guy's apartment. Appears he was a member of a group that called themselves the Brotherhood. Also found instructions he was following to eliminate "the obstacle to peace." I'm guessing that was you. Anyway, bumped up over our heads and Homeland has it. Sorry I wasn't much help. Oh, and here's a weird; his apartment had a bunch of copies of old time tech drawings, that looked to be copies of some of that science fiction stuff you hear about Da Vinci,

Faraday, Tesla and Einstein and stuff; death rays and looked like he was trying to build models. Had them hanging all over the walls. That's when Homeland came in. Look, not supposed to but I took some pictures and am sending them to you for what they're worth. Like I said, he had them hanging all over the walls."

"Thanks. It's going to be interesting. I owe you one or several as the case may be."

Noel hung up and checked his messages, downloading the wall pics. They weren't clear, but he sent them to the others.

"These look like those drawings you delivered to the Smithsonian, some of them, the rest of them? Maybe the same source," remarked Angelica.

"The Brotherhood wants us eliminated?" Noel seemed bemused by the thought. "They sure took long enough to decide that. What have we been fighting them for, a century now? Seems like the roots go way back to that rebellion in San Francisco."

Angelica shook her head. "No, more recent like just before World War 1. I say we up security around your family and try to figure out what all these have in common. There has to be a pattern, How are Violet and the baby?"

"Violet's back at work; baby is in intensive care."

"What!"

"Not the hospital kind. We have him enrolled and are working with his autism with experts. No one can tells us why it happened but it's good that one of the foremost experts on autism is a friend of Violet's and she's there helping out. Baby has a tougher schedule than boot camp. He doesn't seem to me like he's responding but I'm told that takes a lot of time. Violet said he looked t her today, actually looked at her. That's huge for an autistic baby, I guess."

"Hope it goes well."

"I hope it gets calmer. Thanks for the help."

"Remember what grandda used to say?"

"He said a lot of stuff."

"Never give up on a child before they've had a chance to come into themselves. I think he may have something there. Micah's a gift, an odd one, but it might be what we need in the end, You take care, little brother. We'll figure out who these creeps are."

"Thanks Summer. See you at the office soon."

+++

Thank you for reading the second book of The Oberllyn Family's adventures: there are more books to come! In fact, here's a peek at the next book…Rebooting the Oberllyn's is already published and ready for you to read at Amazon. Enjoy the continuing adventure that is the Oberllyn's first seven generations…

Chapter 1

"My Fellow Americans,   now is the time to make the changes we need so desperately in the world - certainly this is not our parent's world. I doubt my Father during his time in office held any idea what would happen just a few years after he retired from this great office; I am certain he thought he had left a lasting legacy of prosperity and peace. Unfortunately, his work was undone by the last elections. We have a chance to bring America back, to make it great again." The crowd erupted in cheers as the candidate finished his opening remarks to the first Presidential debate.

"He talks like his Da," remarked Violet as she sat in her chair crocheting a shawl. She was dressed in her usual quiet dark business suit, with a fresh flower pinned to her lapel. She'd picked it that morning from their balcony flower pots, a single sweetheart rose in pale pink, with its' stem inserted in a tiny bud holder broach, so it wouldn't wilt. Her maroon briefcase lay on the coffee table, mocking the quiet. She figured she could get one more row done before Noel came out of the bedroom and the kids had to be given over to their nanny for the day.

"Not unusual. Our son Kai talks like me," her husband Noel stated as he lay down his newspaper on the table. "I miss our boys." Noel was tall, spare, dressed in a gray pinstriped suit, longish salt and pepper hair combed back behind his ears. His smoky slate eyes glanced at the TV as he sat his maroon briefcase on the coffee table next to his wife's matching case.

"Who's idea was it for them to go into the military after college? And there's more tea in the kitchen and scones." He nodded as he headed for the kitchen.

"I know, I know. They just seemed so young to go into the family business and I had no idea they'd volunteer for this kind of duty. I figured with Kai having that doctorate in genetics and Gabriel his master's in chemistry they'd be headed for some nice research division at skunkworks. They're too young to actually settle down into a life work yet. I mean, Kai is just 24 and Gabe's 20."

"You didn't try to block them with the brass, and you could have," sniffed his wife. "I just hope they come home in one piece."

"We always did."

"We had some awful scrapes over the years."

"Most of them with elected officials now. I'd almost give anything for a good firefight instead of another congressional committee."

"So why didn't you agree to be on the joint chiefs?"

Noel growled at his wife, "Are you out of your mind? How could I keep track of my guys from the sit room?"

"You're in there often enough."

"Yeah, but as a consultant, I have more freedom."

"So where are the boys?"

Noel sighed. "Classified, my dear."

"My security clearance is higher than yours."

"Not with me, it's not."

"Not knowing is killing me."

Noel sat in thought. "I'll just say they aren't in a warm place."

"So not the Middle East then. That leaves only 31 major conflicts. And I know they did not go into the research division as I requested they try for - it's almost like they had to go fight."

"We have good, patriotic sons. They want to do their duty. It is a heritage and tradition in our family to serve in the military. And they will be back in just another two months. Then there is two more years and they're out."

"A lot can happen in two years."

Just then, Jasmine, their daughter called. Her picture popped up on the television screen.

"Hey, mom, guess what? I've been offered an internship at OSU." She smiled. Her long hair was braided over her shoulder, she had dimples and tiny freckles across her nose.

"Really?"

"They really liked my master's thesis. I'm going to work directly under Dr. Franken."

"Marvelous. You'll find him a great guy."

"Don't tell me; he's an old colleague."

"Served in the same psych unit back before you were a twinkle in my eye. He's fair but won't accept shoddy work, so be on your toes."

"Will do, just called to let you know. How's Micah doing?"

"He's learning to cope with his autism. I mean, remember he's just 8."

"Yeah, but those algorithms he was working on..."

"Kai did the same thing at his age. He is bright. He's not untalented. He just can't handle people very well. He can't read social situations; he can't do crowds, he gets anxious easily..."

"I know autism mom, believe me. I did my thesis on it, remember? And having a little brother with it helps with the research."

"Yeah, I keep forgetting you're whizzing through college. You'll always be my little girl sleeping on Grandpa's big bed, wrapped in Grandma's quilt." Jasmine smiled from the screen.

"And besides, Micah is learning to cope: he spends a lot of time dancing."

"Yes, there's that. He's learning the warrior dance for the next powwow."

"He looks so cute in that new regalia."

"Had he not grown so fast, he'd still be in his old regalia. Cute is not how I would describe regalia in the colors he chose, but he is sweet. Spaced out, but sweet."

"Take care. I'll be home for spring council at the land."

"Can't wait to hug you, darling." As she closed the viewer off, Violet sighed. "I wish the boys would call, or write or something."

"They might not be able to do that. They're doing some pretty classified stuff."

"But we have a lot higher security clearance and there's nothing they could possibly be doing that we haven't read briefs on already."

"No, dear. They can't. Trust me. They can't. I'll see what I can learn at the office today."

"And I'm off to argue budgets for Human Services. Sometimes, I think macro practice is just insane. I should have stayed on the state level; the bureaucrats here are enough to make a sane person consider a coup."

"Been through that once, don't intend to do that again. But you do manage them so well."

+++

I do hope you will leave us a review of our books on Amazon: we appreciate it more than you could know! It's really very important to us. God Bless! And I will see you in our next journey.

About the Author:

J. Traveler Pelton was born in West Virginia in the last century. She served as Nation's Mother for her tribe, the Munsee Delaware for eight years: she is wife to Dan (45 years!), Mother of six adults, a grandmother of eight, a Clinically Licensed Independent Social Worker with Supervisory Status, at present in private practice, a retired adjunct professor of social work at her local university and an insatiable reader. She is a cancer survivor. Traveler avidly studies science and technology, fascinated by the inventiveness of people. She is quick to draw parallels in different fields and weave stories around them. Traveler is a fabric artist and her most enjoyable time is spent spinning yarn while spinning yarns for the grandkids…

You can reach Traveler at her website: **travelerpelton.com**

Or on **Facebook at Traveler Pelton**

Or write to her by **snail mail** at

Springhaven Croft
212 Sychar Rd.
Mt. Vernon, OH 43050

She loves to hear from her readers!

All our books are available on Amazon as both eBook and print copy, Kindle unlimited as free downloads and we'd love it if you'd leave us a review!

God bless and see you in our next travels together!

Your Attention Please!!!!

Would you like to join the team at Potpourri Books?

Traveler is <u>always</u> looking for responsible beta readers for her new books. A beta reader gets a prepublication copy of all new books, <u>free of charge</u> in exchange for an honest review written on Amazon, and a short email letting her know of any glitches you may have found that got past the editor, any suggestions you may have, and your opinion of the book. What else do you get out of it?

A beta reader gets:
A free download of one of her already published books
and
as soon as your review of that book gets placed on Amazon,
free downloads of her already published works: for each review, you get a free book.
And
A free copy pre publication copy of all new books...
And
Other neat freebies as they come, from bookmarks to stickers to posters to pens to neat things I find to send out to my betas-
Interested?

Contact Traveler at
travelerpelton@gmail.com for more info...

We would love to add you to the team!

Thanks to those who hurt me,
you made me a stronger person.
Thanks to those who love me,
you made my heart bigger.
Thanks to those who cared,
you made me feel important.
Thanks to those who showed concern,
you let me know that you care.
Thanks to those who left,
you showed me that not everything is forever.
Thanks to those who stayed,
you showed me the true meaning of friendship.
Thanks to those who entered my life,
you helped me become the person I am today.

Old Celtic blessing....

Made in the USA
Middletown, DE
30 January 2022

60027060R00126